❦ BOOK REVIEWS

Here's what people are saying:

Park has done a shrewd job of drawing her characters . . . The humor that has glimmered in her previous novels shines here, and she uses the first-person narrative to the best possible advantage, putting her on a par with (and sometimes above) writers such as Blume and Danziger.

from BOOKLIST

Park offers both wit and a message.

from CHICAGO SUN-TIMES

This uncommonly perceptive story addresses a real problem, dealing with its complexities with sharp humour, admirable characterizations and dialogue, and honesty. . . .

from VERMONT SUNDAY MAGAZINE

ESPECIALLY FOR GIRLS® Presents

BUDDIES

》《

Barbara Park

ALFRED A. KNOPF   NEW YORK

This book is a presentation of **Especially for Girls,**®
Weekly Reader Books. Weekly Reader Books offers
book clubs for children from preschool through high school.
For further information write to: **Weekly Reader Books,**
4343 Equity Drive, Columbus, Ohio 43228.

Published by arrangement with Alfred A. Knopf, Inc.
Especially for Girls and Weekly Reader are federally
registered trademarks of Field Publications.

THIS IS A BORZOI BOOK PUBLISHED BY ALFRED A. KNOPF, INC.

Library of Congress Cataloging in Publication Data
Park, Barbara. Buddies.
Summary: A thirteen-year-old goes to camp yearning
to be popular, but is hampered by an unattractive
cabin mate who wants to be her friend.
1. Children's stories, American.   [1. Camps—Fiction.
2. Friendship—Fiction]   I. Title.
PZ7.P2197Ju 1985 [Fic] 84-12521
ISBN 0-394-86934-6
ISBN 0-394-96934-0 (lib. bdg.)

Especially for Pam,
and also for my brother, Brooke,
who thinks this will make him famous.

BUDDIES

« 1 »

It was ten o'clock on Friday night. I was supposed to have finished packing by eight, but since I was only packing my very nicest clothes, it took a lot of time to separate them from the junk I usually wear. Also, every time I'd finally put something into my duffel bag, my sister, Deena, would pull it out again and say it was hers.

"MOM! SHE'S DOING IT AGAIN!" I screamed for the millionth time. Mother was standing right next to me, but I wanted to emphasize how upset I was.

"It's mine," insisted Deena, hiding my shirt behind her back. "*Isn't* this purple polo mine, Mom? It's the one Aunt Helen gave me for Christmas last year."

My mother shook her head in exasperation. "She gave one to *each* of you."

"I know. But Dinah got some sort of goo all down the front of hers, remember? This one's clean."

It wasn't hard to tell that my mother had really had it with our fighting. She snatched the shirt out of Deena's hands and handed it back to me.

3

"It's hers. I *washed* it. You remember the washer, don't you, Deena? Large white appliance in the laundry room?"

Deena shrugged. "It doesn't matter. I hated that shirt anyway. Purple makes you look like a bruise."

Before she left my room, Deena stuck her tongue out at me. Pretty childish for a fifteen-year-old. I started to go after her, but my mother grabbed me by the back of the collar. I probably would have struggled but she let go and started to rub her temples with her fingers as if she was getting a headache. "If I'd known motherhood was going to be this much fun, I would have had four or five more kids just like you," she told me.

"It's not me . . . it's *her*," I said defensively. "If she had just stayed out of my room, I would have had this done hours ago."

I laid my purple shirt on the top of my other things and carefully pulled the sides of the duffel bag together.

"There. See? All done."

Mother looked at her watch. "Not bad. Only two hours and three minutes behind schedule. I think that's a speed record for you, isn't it?

"Take my advice, Dinah," she continued. "Never get a job bagging groceries. The price of food will go up before you're finished filling your first sack."

"Not funny," I said, keeping a straight face. "*No es* funny, *Madre*." (I took Spanish last year, but we didn't learn the word for funny.)

"How about if you just get in el bedo," said Mom, trying to talk with a Spanish accent. Then she turned

4

down my covers and gave me a warm hug. My mother's the sentimental type. I could tell she didn't like the idea of me going away for two weeks. Once I was under the sheet, she squeezed me again before she turned out the light.

"Get plenty of el sleepo," she said. "You'll need it tomorrow for el campo."

I like my mom a lot, but sometimes when she thinks she's being funny, she keeps it up forever. Later that night, when she went to bed, I heard her tell my dad to let the dog "outsido."

I didn't sleep very well that night. I was nervous. It's embarrassing to admit, but I was thirteen years old, and I had never gone anywhere alone before. Not even for a weekend. I was supposed to fly to St. Louis once to visit a friend who had moved, but I chickened out at the last minute. I was afraid no one would be there to pick me up, and I'd have to live my life at the airport and eat out of trash cans. I realize it sounds stupid now, but I was only eight, and the thought was scary enough to make me want to stick around home for a while.

That's why I was so surprised when I found I wanted to go to camp. The brochure about Camp Miniwawa was posted on the bulletin board at school, and when I read the part about "laughing away the summer days in the cool camp breezes," it sounded so attractive that I took a registration slip home with me that same day. For some reason, being on my own in a place like that really appealed to me.

My parents and I talked it over that night at dinner.

5

At first my father frowned at the price and said it would be cheaper if I just pitched a tent in the backyard for a couple of weeks. I think my mother must have kicked him under the table because by the time we were finished eating, he said I could go.

I didn't shout "Hooray!" or anything. Deena was there, and I didn't want her to know it was that big a deal to me. As a matter of fact, I didn't even tell my best friend, Wanda, how much I wanted to go. I think this was probably part of the reason Wanda kept making fun of the camp. Even when she came over to say good-bye on Saturday morning, she was still making jokes about it.

"Camp Miniwawa," she said, and giggled. "The name just kills me!"

I know I shouldn't have taken her teasing so personally. After all, I wasn't the one who named it. And besides, I knew as well as anyone that Miniwawa was a ridiculous name. But Wanda's joking made me feel like I ought to defend it.

"For your information, Wanda dear," I replied, trying to get an adult tone into my voice, "Miniwawa is an Indian name. It was in the camp brochure. It means . . . ah . . . let's see. . . . Oh, yes. It means 'little water.' "

As soon as the words were out of my mouth, Wanda was rolling on the bed, laughing.

I did my best to ignore her. "Fine. If you don't believe me, ask Tonto. *Mini* means 'little,' and *wawa* means 'water.' "

I wasn't absolutely sure about this. As a matter of fact, I was making it up. And as usual, Wanda didn't believe a word of it. She's a much better liar than I am, which puts me at a disadvantage.

"*Wawa* means 'water'?" she asked, trying to regain her composure. "You're actually going to stand there and tell me that *wawa* is an Indian word? Get serious! My two-year-old brother says *wawa* all the time. 'Mickey want wawa!'"

I put my hand on her shoulder. "You must be very proud of Mickey . . . only two and already speaking Indian."

Wanda punched me playfully on the arm. "Relax. Just because it has a stupid name doesn't mean it's a stupid camp. My blobby cousin Henry went to camp last year. It was only a day camp, but he really liked it. Each camper got to wear a headband with a feather in it, so Henry thought it made him part Indian or something. They called him Big Chief Little Squirt. The rest of the summer, every time he'd skin his knee, he'd try to make you his blood brother. The kid's an idiot."

From the opposite end of the hall, I heard my sister's door slam. "Yeah," I sympathized. "But unfortunately, we can't pick our relatives."

Wanda and I listened as Deena's footsteps got closer and closer to my room. Seconds later, she stuck her head in my doorway, then barged right in.

"Perfect example," I muttered. "If I had my choice, *that* one would be the first to go."

7

Deena ignored the comment and tossed her hair in the air. It's a new annoying habit of hers. She must think she's in a shampoo commercial.

"Aren't you gone yet?" she moaned.

"Yeah, I'm gone, Deena," I replied sarcastically. "I left two hours ago. You're actually standing here talking to my bed."

She looked at her watch and tossed her hair again. "It's almost nine fifteen. I thought your bus left at ten."

"Ten thirty," I corrected. "But I've been waiting for *you* to leave. Wanda and I wanted to browse around in your room awhile in case there's anything else of yours I might want to take with me."

Deena's eyes got as big as saucers. "Else? I *knew* you had some of my belongings in that little nylon sack!"

I smiled slyly and winked at Wanda. "Don't worry. She'll never miss it."

"MOTHERRRR! DINAH'S GOT SOMETHING OF MINE! MOTHERRRR!"

Finally, she stopped yelling and went away, to do her tattling face to face. Personally, I think Deena has gone off the deep end when it comes to her clothes. If there was a fire in our house, she'd probably save her sweat socks before she'd save me. But what can you expect from a person who calls her stuff "belongings"?

The two of us are nothing alike. Normally, I don't pay much attention to what I'm wearing. Camp was going to be special, so I made an exception; but usually I'll put on almost anything. I think it started when

8

Deena began giving me her hand-me-downs. When my relatives found out I'd wear old clothes, they dumped their old stuff on me too. I guess I could have said no thanks, but I didn't want to hurt their feelings. Now, whenever anyone in the neighborhood feels guilty about throwing something away, they automatically give it to me instead. "Good old Dinah Feeney will get some use out of it," they say.

"Taking this?"

From behind me, Wanda appeared, wearing my poodle hat. When she saw herself in the mirror, she started to bark.

Irritated, I snatched it off her head. My aunt Maude made it for me years ago. It's gray with these ridiculous long ears hanging down the sides. They're curly. I don't know how you knit curly, but trust me, Aunt Maude did it.

I probably should have gotten rid of it a long time ago. But every time I try to throw it away, I get this picture in my head of Aunt Maude sitting all alone in her apartment, knitting it for me. It's made me feel so guilty, I actually put it on my head when she comes to visit. I don't keep it on long. But even so, when you're wearing a poodle hat, time passes very slowly.

"Okay then, how about these?" asked Wanda again, pulling something else from my closet floor.

Dangling them by their dirty laces, she tried to keep from cracking up. "If I've said it once, I've said it a thousand times. It's always good to have an old pair of black ice-hockey skates handy. You never know when

9

the Chicago Black Hawks are going to breeze through town looking for a new goalie."

"Put them back," I commanded. Between Wanda and Deena, I was losing my patience. "Mrs. Trebolina gave them to me. They used to be Freddie's."

Wanda rolled her eyes. "For Pete's sake, Dinah! You're such a sucker! Freddie Trebolina is at least twenty years old. These things are practically antiques! Why didn't you just tell her you didn't want them?"

"I couldn't. She looked so happy to have found them a home. You should have heard her telling me how much they had cost and how Freddie hadn't amounted to a hill of beans as a hockey player. The second time he wore them, he took a puck in the nose, and they'd been in her basement ever since."

Wanda made a face. "Wearing black hockey skates is like wearing your father's shoes to school."

I guess she could tell by the way I was glaring at her that I was getting annoyed. I didn't even have to ask. She just opened the closet door and put the skates back.

For a few seconds the two of us stood there gazing inside. Besides the piles of old clothes, there were secondhand coats, jackets, boots, and two bags of other people's old Halloween costumes. I don't really plan to go trick-or-treating anymore, but if I change my mind, I can be anything from Mr. Peanut to a bottle of ketchup.

Leaning up against the back wall of the closet was

my campaign poster from the fourth grade. The giant red stenciled letters stared us in the face.

GRADE FOUR NEEDS . . .
DINAH FEENEY—THE KIND ONE

"Dinah Feeney, The Sucker, is more like it," said Wanda, scratching her head. "You never told me that you ran for office."

"Yeah. It was right before you moved here."

"Did you win?"

I tried to look casual. "No. But I was very kind to everyone who voted against me."

Wanda looked at the slogan a little longer. "Maybe you needed a saying with a little more zip to it. Something to pep up your image," she offered at last. "Let's see. How about . . . Dinah Feeney, She's No Wienie."

This time when I glared, Wanda decided to go home. When you've known someone for four years, you can usually tell when it's time to depart.

On her way out the door, she made me promise not to forget her. Wanda doesn't have many friends, so she gets a little panicky when I'm not available.

As soon as she was gone, I sat down on the edge of my bed and stared into my closet some more. Once in a while it bothers me to see how much junk I've taken from other people. Sometimes I wish I could learn to say no. Being kind really *can* make you look like a sucker.

11

I don't know where I got all my kindness. It doesn't seem to run in the family. If it did, my parents would have been kind enough not to have had Deena.

It was almost time to leave. I went outside to say good-bye to Rollo. I guess even my dog is secondhand. The Clayborns gave him to me a few years ago when they moved. By the time I got him, Rollo was so old it was plain to see that his romping days were over. I don't want to sound mean, but having Rollo is a lot like having an old man for a pet.

He's crotchety, and he limps, and a lot of his hair's falling out, but I love him more than anything. Old dogs just seem to need more kindness than others.

"I should have known you were out here with Stinky."

Looking up, I saw Deena standing on the steps of the back porch. Quickly I covered Rollo's ears.

"He *knows* when you call him that, Deena," I said. "Being old doesn't make you stupid."

Deena put her hands over her face and shook her head. "You're getting weirder by the minute," she muttered.

"The fact that I love something besides myself doesn't make me a weirdo," I snapped.

Deena paused a minute. "It's not just Rollo you're weird about," she replied at last. "If it were only the dog, there would be no problem. The trouble is, you've turned out to be weird about everything. Just look at you, Dinah. Your best friend's a drip, you wear Nana's sweaters, and whenever Aunt Maude comes over, you run around wearing a gray hat with poodle ears. You don't think *that's* weird?"

"It's called protecting people's feelings, Deena. Something you know nothing about."

"What about *my* feelings?" she retorted. "Think about how embarrassing it is having a nerd for a sister."

I smiled smugly and looked up. "Who needs to think? I've got one, remember?"

Deena made a move toward me, but just as she closed in, Rollo sat up suddenly and threw a little slobber on her leg. You could hear her *"UGH!"* all over the neighborhood. Then, just to show how insensitive she is, she leaned down into Rollo's tired old face and told him that he smelled.

I hated it when she said that. Especially because it was true. Not just the part about Rollo smelling. *Everything* was true. Even the part about Wanda.

I don't mean that she's a drip. She's not. But to put it nicely, Wanda Freeman is not exactly the most popular kid in school. How can you be popular when your favorite singing group is the Vienna Boys' Choir? Also, she looks a teeny bit like Howard Cosell. They have the same hairstyle.

Don't get me wrong. I wouldn't trade Wanda for any other friend in the world. But still, the truth is that hanging around with a girl like that doesn't exactly speed you along the road to popularity. She's sort of like my poodle hat. Even though she may be warm and comfortable, if you're trying to impress anyone, it's probably better to leave her in the closet.

13

It makes me feel guilty even to think such a thing. When we chose each other as friends, no one told us that looks were important. What was I supposed to do—tell her I was sorry, but she just didn't grow up cute enough?

It's not that I wouldn't like to be as popular as my sister. Deena makes it look like so much fun, I'd be crazy not to want it for myself. Ever since I started school, I've wondered what it would be like to have the other kids say hi to me just so I would say hi back. It must be a nice feeling to be able to pal around with the big shots of the school. They seem to have a better time than the rest of us. Deena's always dashing to some party or other. That's what she calls it, dashing. "See ya! Gotta dash!" she'll say.

Wanda and I don't do much dashing. Actually we spend most of our school time just trying to stay out of other people's way. I guess that's how it is. Popular kids dash. The rest of us dodge.

Deep down, I think that's the main reason I was looking forward to going to Miniwawa. I was thirteen years old, and I was sick and tired of doing all the dodging. Camp seemed to be a way to change all that for a while. After all, no one would know me there. Not one person would know that I had black hockey skates in my closet. We would all be starting out as strangers. I could be almost anything I wanted to be. Maybe even popular.

Deena didn't know it, but she helped me reach my final decision. By the time she went into the house that morning, my mind was made up. If she was right . . . if I really *was* getting weirder by the minute, then maybe it was time to lock my poodle hat in the closet once and for all and start looking out for myself. Camp would only last two weeks. And maybe, just maybe, it was time for me to see what all the dashing was about.

«2»

Campers were supposed to be at the bus stop at ten thirty on Saturday morning. I arrived at nine fifty-five. I probably don't have to mention that this made me the first one there. The buses hadn't even arrived yet.

It was my mother's fault. No matter what the occasion may be, if Mother has anything to do with it, we're always the first ones there. If you ask me, she has some sort of mental problem about being late. I talked to my father about it once, but he seemed to think she just has a poor sense of timing. It's easy for him to say. *He* wasn't the one who showed up the first day of kindergarten before the school building was even opened. When the janitor finally came, he called me an eager beaver. What a humiliating way to begin your education.

It never does any good to argue with her. We still end up going early. The only difference arguing makes is that I have to listen to her Promptness Is a Virtue speech. I have a feeling it's the same speech the Early

Bird's mother used right before she made him eat his first worm.

Deena didn't go to the bus stop with us. She said she didn't think she liked me enough to miss Saturday morning TV. It didn't break my heart. I put my duffel bag in her place, and it didn't say one mean thing the entire trip.

While we were standing there waiting for the buses to come, my father told me I looked nice. Dad seems to take a lot of pride in his family. Some men would probably rather have sons than daughters, but I don't think my father minds. He's not really the athletic type. He tried to throw a football at a family reunion once, and it went in the potato salad.

I look more like him than like my mother. Dad and I both have brown hair and blue eyes. Normally, *brown* eyes go with brown hair, so people are always telling me I have unusual coloring. It drives Deena crazy when I get a compliment like that. She says I'm a human oddity.

I guess what I'm really trying to say is that I'm not bad looking. As a matter of fact, the word for me might even be *cute*. I'd never use it, of course. Never in a million years. When you have a girl friend who looks like Howard Cosell, there are certain things you learn never to discuss. Being cute is one of them. Hairstyles are another. . . .

Wanda was not with me now, though, and I had to put her out of my thoughts. The time had come to concentrate on becoming a member of the "in" crowd, and the wait was beginning to make me nervous.

"What time is it anyway?" I asked at last. "Where *is* everybody?"

"They'll be here," retorted my mother defensively. "Just keep your pants on."

I hate it when she says "Keep your pants on." I wasn't planning to take my pants off. I was just wondering why no one else was there yet, that's all.

At that moment, we were all surprised by the sound of a car backfiring, and I turned to see a huge old automobile pulling into the parking lot. It wasn't a Cadillac, but it was enormous, metallic blue with these giant fins on the back. My father whistled and said he hadn't seen one of those babies in years.

The three of us watched curiously as it slowly rambled toward us, finally coming to a stop a few feet from where we were standing.

It sat there a minute or two before a heavy woman got out of the driver's seat. She was wearing a T-shirt that read I LOVE MY BULLDOG. Only it didn't have the words *love* or *bulldog*. It had a red heart and a dog picture.

Even from where we were standing, I could see the woman was wearing bright red lipstick, and she had her hair in a big pile on her head. I know there's probably a name for the style, but "big pile" describes it pretty well.

She smiled in our direction and opened the back door. Since the car windows were tinted almost black,

18

this was the first time I realized there was someone else in the car. I didn't get a good look, though. As soon as the door was opened, whoever was inside quickly pulled it shut and locked it.

You could tell the woman was embarrassed. She kept looking at us and giggling as she tried to figure out what to do next. My father told me not to stare. He said Mother was staring enough for both of us.

Finally, the woman gave the person in the back seat a roll-down-the-window signal. Then, as the window was slowly lowered, she stuck her lips close to the opening and delivered some kind of message. I'm pretty sure it was a death threat, because a few seconds later the door opened and a girl got out.

She was a little bit overweight, and her straight brown hair hung down in her eyes. She had on a white T-shirt with red shorts and suspenders. I think the suspenders were supposed to look stylish, but the outfit looked like something Mickey Mouse might wear.

The mother giggled again and pulled the girl's duffel bag out of the car. "She's a shy one," she said, shaking her head.

Typically, my mother nodded in agreement and pointed her finger at my back. "We've got one too," she replied.

I hate it when she does stuff like that. For some reason, parents seem to feel they all have to stick together. I'm sure if the woman had said, "She's a real chowderhead," my mother would have smiled politely and said, "Yes, we have a chowderhead too."

After setting the large bag next to mine, the woman stuck out her hand and said, "I'm Ilsa Davis. How'ja do?"

My mother shook it first, then my father. When she moved it toward me, it took me by surprise. "I do fine," I blurted foolishly as she pumped my arm up and down.

The woman giggled again and gave me a pat on the head. "It looks like these two are going to be campmates," she remarked to my parents. "What's 'er name?"

"Dinah," offered my father.

"This one's Fern," she announced, giving her daughter a squeeze. "Fern Wadley. Last name's different. Had her by my second hubby. I'm on my third now."

This time when she laughed, it wasn't a giggle. It was real deep and hearty, almost like a man's.

The girl rolled her eyes but Ilsa didn't seem to notice.

Looking down at her daughter and me, she grinned. "I wonder if the two of you could say hello to each other. I think that would be nice. Don't you, Mom and Dad?"

My parents nodded sheepishly.

I couldn't believe this was really happening. I felt like I was on *Mr. Rogers' Neighborhood*. Next to me, my mother was nudging me in the side. On the fourth nudge I finally said, "Hi."

Fern didn't say anything back. She just swallowed hard and started to sweat. Her oily skin started breaking

20

out in red blotches. Nerves, I guess. A mother like that would make anyone nervous.

Even so, I knew the girl's attitude was driving my mother crazy. Mother's what you'd call the social type. She likes to put everyone at ease right away. At parties she's the lady who goes around with the cracker tray, trying to get people to talk to one another. It's one of the main reasons I've never had a party.

Hoping to get her to say a few words, my mother smiled. "How old are you, Fern?" she asked.

"Twelve and a third," chimed Ilsa. "Be thirteen March eleventh. Why? How old's DeeDee?"

My father frowned. "It's Dinah. She's thirteen."

Meanwhile, Mother was becoming more determined than ever to make Fern talk. "Do you have any brothers or sisters at home, dear?" she questioned, leaning closer.

Ilsa let out another hearty roar. "You kidding? It's hard enough with just one. Who do I look like . . . the old woman in the shoe?"

My parents laughed politely.

"We're hoping camp'll bring 'er out of her shell a little bit," she continued. "My hubby says I talk so much, Fern doesn't have a chance to get a word in edgewise." Then she tweaked her daughter on the cheek. "I hope you don't get a sore throat from all the talkin' you're going to be doing."

Judging from the petrified look on Fern's face, I didn't think it would be a problem.

Even though it was obvious that Fern was annoyed

21

at her mother for sending her to camp, when the buses finally rolled in, she hugged her for about ten minutes. Ilsa had to pull Fern's arms off her. "Go on now, Fernie. Just stay with DeeDee. She'll show you where to go."

I thought I would die. Frantically, I turned to my parents and gave them my I-don't-want-to-sit-with-her look.

I should have known better. Most parents are too old to remember teenage desperation. Mother just leaned down and pretended to give me a hug while she whispered in my ear, "It won't *kill* you to be nice to her." Then, before I had a chance to argue, she rushed the two of us to the buses so we would be first in line.

Fern got right on board. Meanwhile, Mother and Dad both began hugging me at the same time, making a spectacle of themselves. They're both pretty emotional about good-byes.

When they finally let go, I waved from the doorway and reluctantly sat down next to Fern. I wasn't crazy about the seat she'd picked. It was right behind the driver and I've ridden enough buses to know that unless the driver's wearing a clown suit, there's a good chance he's not going to be a lot of fun.

This one was dressed in black. He was round, but that's about as close as he came to looking jolly. When he sat down, he told me not to kick the back of his seat.

I was pretty surprised at how quickly the bus filled up. At first I was worried that most of the girls had come with a friend. But after everyone was seated, the bus was so quiet, it made me think a lot of them had just met in the parking lot. I was relieved to think we were all in the same boat.

It wasn't long at all before we pulled out of the parking lot. And I have to admit, I was pretty happy to finally get moving. Ever since I had gotten on board, my mother had been standing outside my window pressing her palm against the glass. I think it's nice that she cares so much about me, but sometimes I wish she'd keep it a little more private.

Even after we were on the road, the girls on the bus were a pretty lifeless group. I hate to say it, but the driver turned out to be the liveliest guy on board. At the end of the first street, he picked up a microphone lying next to his seat and began to talk.

"Good morning, ladies," he said cheerfully. "This is Bernard speaking. The temperature outside is seventy-six degrees and the sun is shining. We expect the sunshine to continue until we arrive at our final destination, Camp Miniwawa."

It was like Bernard thought he was a pilot. He even started naming all the famous places we would pass on our way to camp. I have lived in Illinois all my life, and I had never heard of any of them.

After Bernard finished his little speech, he decided to try to pep things up a bit with a song.

Ninety-nine bottles of beer on the wall,
Ninety-nine bottles of beerrrrr . . .

If one of those bottles should happen to fall,
Ninety-eight bottles of beer on the wall. . . .

Bernard was really belting it into the microphone. It was one of the most embarrassing displays I have ever witnessed. When he got down to ninety-five, he finally realized that no one was going to join him, so he stopped. He wasn't a very good sport about it. He said that driving our bus was like driving a herd of cattle to slaughter.

Fern continued to sit quietly and stare out the window. I knew she was probably scared to death of what would happen when we got to camp. I was actually a little nervous myself. But I made myself relax, knowing I had a plan of action. . . .

First of all, when I got off the bus, I would be on the lookout for anyone who seemed like the popular type. I was sure they wouldn't be hard to find. Most popular kids are born with the ability to call attention to themselves. After that, it would just be a matter of hanging around them a lot until I zoomed to popularity right along with them.

Fern wasn't in my plan. I felt sorry for her, of course. *Really* sorry. But I didn't think it was fair for her to become my responsibility. After all, if I was ever going to start looking out for my image, I couldn't begin by dragging Fern Wadley around with me. I knew Ilsa and her hubby wanted her to come out of her shell. But that didn't mean I had to be the one to pull her, did it?

I looked at Fern again. She looked so uptight and nervous, just sitting next to her gave me the willies.

I knew my mother would have been ashamed of me for not speaking. "It won't *kill* you to be nice to her" went through my mind at least a thousand times.

Oh, all right! I thought at last. I'll try to get her to relax a little, but that's *all* I'm going to do. Just a couple of simple questions to break the ice. . . .

I took a deep breath and thought over what I would say. Then, clearing my throat, I tapped her on the shoulder. Fern jumped about a foot.

"You have any hobbies?"

I realized I had taken her by surprise, so I waited patiently for a reply. But instead of answering, she just sat there for five minutes wiping sweat beads off her top lip.

Normally, being ignored like that would have made me mad. But Fern was in such bad shape, I decided to give her another chance. This time I was a little more forceful.

"I ASKED IF YOU HAD ANY HOBBIES."

This time she started shaking her head from side to side so quickly it made me dizzy just to watch. Hoping to get her to stop, I moved on to my second question.

"How 'bout pets? I've got a secondhand dog named Rollo and a goldfish named Filthy. My mother named it. Also, I used to have one of those small diseased turtles, but my parents made me take him back to the store."

25

Fern made a face and turned back toward the window.

"How 'bout *your* pets? I guess you have a bulldog, huh?"

Fern wiped her upper lip again, fidgeted a minute, and finally opened her mouth to speak.

"No, I don't," she replied meekly.

"But . . . your mother had a shirt with 'I love my bulldog' on it."

"It was on sale."

"Oh."

After that I didn't ask any more questions. I had done my best to be nice. I had even gotten her to speak.

But even though I still felt sorry for her, it was pretty clear that Fern Wadley and I had nothing in common. The truth is, I don't even sweat much. Once in a while, if it's really hot outside, maybe . . . but I don't ever really drip.

We were almost to camp, and it was time for me to start becoming the new Dinah Feeney. Dinah Feeney—The Popular One. And just as soon as Bernard opened the bus doors, it was going to be every girl for herself.

« 3 »

The final road to Miniwawa was a long narrow trail that wound through the woods. As we drove, branches from bordering pine trees brushed against my window. Going that deep into the forest didn't worry me, exactly, but I think I would have felt more comfortable if we had stayed a little closer to civilization. For some reason, the wilderness doesn't seem quite as threatening if there's a McDonald's in walking distance.

After about thirty minutes of winding roads and pine trees, we came to a clearing. In front of us I could see a small parking lot and, beyond that, a giant log cabin. At the entrance was a large girl wearing a worn-out Indian headdress and a sign that read HEAP BIG WELCOME TO NEW CAMPERS!!! As my father says, some people will do anything for a buck.

Bernard pulled into the parking lot and waited for the other buses to join him before he opened the doors. He still wasn't speaking, so we weren't given any instructions; but when Bernard stood up to stretch his legs, the whole bus stood up with him. All except Fern, that is. She was so busy chewing her nails and sweating, I don't think she noticed the commotion around her.

Outside, I could see a dozen different counselors lined up, holding clipboards and pencils. Most of them looked pretty young, about nineteen or twenty. A lot of them were frowning, probably trying to look more grown-up. Suddenly one of them raised and lowered her hand and all the bus doors opened at once, as if she were Moses. Then, one by one, we all began filing into the parking lot.

As I started off the bus I felt a tug on the back of my shirt. At first I didn't think anything about it, but as I hit the first step, I realized it was more than just a little tug. Fern had grabbed the bottom of my shirt and was holding on tightly. I felt like I was leading an elephant parade.

I wanted to tell her to let go, but before I had a chance, the counselor outside the door leaned in and hollered, "MOVE IT!"

Quickly jumping to the ground, I pulled Fern with me. Unfortunately, she was a little slow, and my shirt stretched about a mile and a half. I tried swatting her hand away, but I missed.

"Name and age!" the counselor blasted in my ear.

"Er . . . ah . . . Dinah Feeney, thirteen," I answered nervously.

"Fine. And who's this trying to pull your shirt off?"

I turned around and we both stared at Fern, waiting

for her to answer. She tried, but when she opened her mouth, nothing came out.

The counselor frowned and leaned closer. "YOU NO SPEAKIE DE ENGLISH OR WHAT?" she yelled.

Fern's grip on my shirt tightened.

This time the counselor held up her hand. "Don't tell me . . . let me guess. You're Siamese twins joined at the shirttail."

Furious at Fern for putting me in this position, I took a deep breath. "Her name's Fern Wadley, and she was twelve last March eleventh."

The counselor bowed from the waist. "Thank you, Miss Feeney. And now I suppose you'll tell me that you and your friend want to be in the same cabin?"

"Well . . . ah, no . . . I mean, that's not really necessary or anything. The thing is, we're not really friends. Our mothers just met at the bus stop, see, and—"

"Cabin eleven."

"Er . . . excuse me?"

"Cabin eleven," she repeated. "I put you both in cabin eleven."

"Yes . . . but see, the thing is, we don't *have* to be in the same—"

"CABIN ELEVEN, FEENEY! MOVE IT!"

Camp might be in the peaceful forest, but it was loud. Very loud.

Fern didn't let go of me until we got our duffel bags from Bernard. Fortunately, hers was so bulky, she needed both hands just to drag it across the ground. It wasn't like the cute nylon duffel bags most of the rest of us had. It was a huge green canvas thing, the kind a marine would use.

As the two of us stood in line behind the cabin 11 sign, I tried to ignore the sound of Fern gasping for breath and concentrate on what was going on around me. It didn't take long to discover that the camp was divided into age groups. The youngest group, six- to eight-year-olds, were called the Daffy Ducklings. Stupid, I know, but it only gets worse. The nine- to eleven-year-olds were the Ever-Greenies. And *my* age group, the twelve- to fourteen-year-olds, were called the Awesome Possums.

I don't know why camps insist on making fun of the campers this way, but they all do it. Until that moment, Big Chief Little Squirt was the most demeaning thing I had ever heard. Now that I've been an Awesome Possum, it doesn't sound that bad.

I'm not sure how many cabins the other age groups had, but ours had six. Each cabin was supposed to have eight campers plus a counselor. None of them were filled, though. In fact, our cabin only ended up with five.

The third girl assigned to our group was named Crystal. I didn't have a yardstick with me, but offhand I'd say Crystal was about ten feet tall. Her last name was Ball, but after you saw the size of her, you weren't even tempted to laugh. When she lined up behind us, Fern started gasping harder than ever.

The fourth girl to join us was tall and tan. She was what my grandmother would call "a real character." She was wearing a shirt that read I'D RATHER BE DEAD. Instead of telling the counselor her name and age, she asked to call her lawyer. I thought this was a pretty funny thing to say. The counselor didn't laugh, but she seemed to know her and pushed her toward us.

The next girl in line was almost too good to be true. It was almost as if she was wearing a sign that said *I'm one of those popular ones*. Everything about her looked perfect: perfect hair, perfect clothes, perfect smile. She even had a perfect voice.

"Cassandra Barnhill," she said confidently. "I'll be fourteen in six weeks."

The counselor stared at her for a moment. "How very wonderful for you, Cassandra," she said at last. "I'll be sixty-seven in forty-eight years, but right now that makes me nineteen, doesn't it?"

Cassandra didn't even look embarrassed. She just picked up her things.

"Cabin eleven," said the counselor, and Cassandra headed toward our group.

Normally, I'm not a lucky person. That's why I couldn't believe it when Cassandra Barnhill was assigned to my cabin. I was so thrilled, I practically ran out to hug her. I could tell just by looking at her that she was exactly the kind of girl I had come to camp to meet. Her hair was auburn. At least that's what I think they call it when it's reddish brown. It was thick and shiny and came down to the middle of her back. She was wearing expensive-looking hiking shorts and two polo shirts. Two. One on top of the other. Before Cassandra, I had only seen that sort of thing on store mannequins. *Both* her collars were turned up.

Naturally, it takes more than just clothes to make you popular. After all, if that's all it took, Wanda and I would have turned up our collars a long time ago. But more than the way she dressed, Cassandra had a certain look about her that really set her apart. I'm not sure what it's called, but it was very clear that before we left, Cassandra Barnhill was going to be one of the most popular girls at camp.

And if I have *my* way, Dinah Feeney is going to be right next to her, I thought happily. There was no better time to make my first move.

I smiled.

She smiled back. It was nice to know that wearing two polos didn't make her unfriendly.

"Hi," I said, getting bolder.

"Hi," she said back.

"Is this your first time here?"

Cassandra looked a little disgusted. "It was Pop's idea. It's one of those things he never got to do as a kid, so now he's sticking me with it."

I smiled again. *Pop.* I liked that. Maybe I'd start calling my father *Pop* too.

The girl who had asked for her lawyer leaned into the conversation. "Talk about getting stuck," she growled. "I've been coming to this armpit since I was six. My grandfather helped start the place, so I don't have much choice. The camp was practically named after him." She reached her hand out. "Let me introduce myself. I'm Marilyn Wawa."

No one laughed except Marilyn. That's because no one else knew it was a joke. Actually, the *name* was a joke, but the rest of what she said turned out to be true. Her real name was Marilyn Powers, and her grandfather really *was* the founder of Camp Miniwawa. She said he had put up the money, but had nothing to do with the name.

"I try to get out of coming here every year," she said bluntly. "But what can you do? I get in for free, and I'm a brat, so it's too good a deal for my parents to pass up."

"ATTENTION, CABIN ELEVEN! COULD ALL OF YOU LISTEN UP FOR A MOMENT, PLEASE? MY NAME IS MAGGIE BLOCKER, AND I'M GOING TO BE YOUR COUNSELOR FOR THE NEXT TWO WEEKS."

Marilyn leaned toward me and whispered into my ear, "Correct me if I'm wrong, but isn't Maggie short for Maggot?"

Cassandra and I began to laugh, only by then she had told me to call her just Cass. Maggie Blocker squinted her eyes and waited for us to stop. She had the kind of beady eyes that looked like they could shoot laser beams.

"RIGHT NOW WE'RE GOING TO BE HEADING FOR OUR CABIN. AFTER YOU'VE SELECTED A BUNK, WE'LL HAVE A SHORT

TOUR OF THE CAMPGROUNDS. ARE THERE ANY QUESTIONS?"

"I HAVE ONE," bellowed Marilyn, shooting up her hand. "WHY ARE WE ALL SHOUTING?"

Maggie was not amused. She glared a few seconds and then told Marilyn, "I've got your number." I don't know exactly what it means when someone has your number, but I have a feeling it's a lot like the old saying, "You're dead meat."

After that, Maggie turned and gave us the signal to follow her. It was the same signal they use on Westerns when the wagon train pulls out. Behind me, Marilyn muttered, "Wagons ho."

We really didn't need a guide to find our area. The trail was clearly marked by signs with gross little possums hanging by their tails. Marilyn said she recognized a few of them as former campers.

Although it was only a short hike to the cabin, some of us made it quicker than others. Crystal didn't make it at all. "Tell what's-'er-face I'll be along later," she said in a husky voice.

Fern made it, but just barely. Her duffel bag was giving her trouble. Since it was large and awkward to carry, she couldn't sling it over her shoulder the way the rest of us did. Instead, she'd drag it a few minutes and then sit down on top of it to wheeze awhile. I'm not sure, but I have a feeling that lugging heavy duffel bags is one of the ways Marines Build Men.

My mother would have been proud. Somehow I

34

managed to be the first one inside cabin 11. I could hear Maggie, outside, issuing instructions to the others: "PICK OUT A BUNK AND THROW YOUR BAGS ON TOP. WE'LL WORRY ABOUT UNPACKING AFTER THE TOUR!"

Since there were only two people standing there, I don't know why she was still shouting. But something told me she thought she'd been hired as a drill sergeant.

Marilyn already knew the procedure by heart and tossed her stuff on the first bed she came to. "What's the difference where you bunk?" she said with a shrug. "You can't sleep in this rathole anyway."

Even so, I decided to be a little more selective, and I took my time. The truth is, I had another plan. . . .

Since I had already chosen Cassandra to be my best friend, it was only natural that I wait to see where she was going to sleep. Then, once she had decided on a bed, I would casually stroll over and place my things on the bunk directly on top or below. Best friends are almosts *always* bunkmates, I thought, smiling slyly to myself.

Putting my plan into action, I cleverly knelt down and fiddled with my bag while Cass stalked the room looking over each and every bed. I think she was trying to find the mattress with the fewest stains.

Unfortunately, as I was waiting, the cabin door slammed behind me and the sound of wheezing filled the room. I didn't have to turn around to know it was Fern. She was huffing and puffing worse than the big bad wolf. Hoping to avoid her gaze, I crouched lower and prayed Cassandra would hurry and make up her mind.

Suddenly, I felt a sweaty finger tap the back of my neck. I knew it was all over. When I looked up, Fern was hovering above me, still trying to catch her breath. Her face was red as a beet; her arms hung limply at her sides.

As I stared upward, a drop from her chin hit my face. "Where are we going to sleep?" she muttered.

I was dead. No one could save me. Marilyn was already outside, and Cassandra was still making faces at every mattress she came to. Why was she making such a big deal about a few lousy stains? What difference did it make? You couldn't sleep in this rathole anyway!

By this time, Fern had dragged her load to the closest available bunk and stood wearily at its side. Glancing over at me with raised eyebrows, she pointed first to the upper and then to the lower. She didn't actually say anything, but the message was clear: top or bottom?

Reluctantly, I picked my things up off the cabin floor and threw them on the top bunk. Fern nodded her approval and flopped on the bottom bed to finish wheezing.

I covered my face with my hands and shook my head. Bunkmates were *almost* always best friends . . . but the rest of the time, they weren't.

« 4 »

Maggie Blocker was not nearly as big as her voice. I'm not very good at estimating people's height, but of all the counselors, she was definitely the shortest. She was also the most muscular; not fat, really—just sort of stocky-looking. If you've ever seen a women's midget wrestling match, you probably know the look I'm trying to describe.

Her hair was short and dark, and she wore an earring in one ear. I thought she was trying to be cool, but later I found out she had just lost the other one. Her face was covered with freckles, which she didn't bother trying to hide with makeup the way Deena does.

Maggie was going to be a junior in college, majoring in physical education. You could tell she was really eager to become a gym teacher. She had already learned to talk with a whistle in her mouth. While we were inside choosing our bunks, she stood outside the door blowing her whistle as loud as she could. It took about ten minutes before it finally dawned on her that we weren't paying any attention.

"ARE YOU GUYS DEAF?" she shouted at last, as she angrily yanked the screen door open and peered inside. "DIDN'T ANY OF YOU HEAR ME BLOWING?"

In the corner I heard Fern shuffle her feet nervously. Maggie didn't notice.

"FROM NOW ON, WHEN I BLOW MY WHISTLE, I WANT YOU TO COME RUNNING. IS THAT UNDERSTOOD? I TOOT AND YOU RUN!"

"How degrading," murmured Cassandra.

Outside, the girls from the other cabins were already assembling for the tour. Although their counselors were with them, Maggie Blocker had been selected to be the tour guide. I don't think it was any kind of honor, though. She was the only one who didn't need a bullhorn to be heard.

The tour of the campgrounds took about an hour and a half. It really was a beautiful place—lots of birds and lakes and streams and wooden bridges. I couldn't help thinking how much my grandfather would have enjoyed some of the trails. Sometimes when he comes to visit, I take walks with him. He's slow, but he gets pleasure out of looking at the things around him. He says he's at the age when a person should "stop and smell the roses." It's an adult expression, but I think I know what it means.

I don't think Miniwawa would have tired him out too much. It wasn't as big as it looked in the brochure. I'm sure we could have toured it quicker if there hadn't been so many rules and regulations to explain at each stop.

I tried to stay close to Cassandra so she would get the idea that we were becoming pals, but Fern didn't make it easy. She walked so close behind me that twice she stepped on the backs of my tennis shoes. I think she was afraid of getting left behind in the woods. She was the only girl on the tour who brought a canteen and a compass.

When we got to the lake, the group stopped unexpectedly, and Fern walked right into my back. Marilyn turned around and called her a lummox. It was supposed to be a joke, but since Fern didn't have a sense of humor, it ended up more like an insult. Marilyn didn't seem to feel bad about it, though. You could tell she hadn't come to camp to make a lot of new friends.

Meanwhile, near the shore, Maggie had begun spouting off the rules of the lake. The first rule was No Swimming.

"I REPEAT . . . NO SWIMMING UNLESS YOU ARE SCHEDULED FOR IT! EACH MORNING YOU WILL SIGN UP FOR THE ACTIVITIES YOU PLAN TO PARTICIPATE IN THAT DAY. IF SWIMMING IS ONE OF YOUR CHOICES, YOU WILL BE REQUIRED TO TAKE A SWIMMING TEST. THERE WILL BE SWIMMING LESSONS FOR THOSE OF YOU WHO SINK.

"THE REST OF YOU ARE REQUIRED TO SWIM WITH A BUDDY. EVERY TEN MINUTES

A WHISTLE WILL BLOW. YOU MUST THEN GRAB THE HAND OF YOUR BUDDY AND HOLD IT IN THE AIR. ANYONE COMING UP WITHOUT A HAND WILL LOSE HER SWIMMING PRIVILEGES!"

"Not to mention a great deal of blood," added Marilyn quietly.

After the swimming area, the tour continued to the boat dock, then the stables, the archery range, and the arts-and-crafts center. At each stop Marilyn added her own personal comments about what we were seeing.

"You'll love the crafts you get to make," she said as we toured the supply room. "They come in two categories: ugly stuff you can make for yourself and ugly stuff you can make for those you love. Last year I made each member of my family a plaster gorilla. My mother waited until Christmas and then gave them to the needy." The three of us laughed all the way back to the cabin.

By the time we got there, it was almost one thirty. Fern wasn't far behind. She had stopped to take a sip from her canteen, so at least she was no longer right on my heels.

When we went inside, Crystal was on her bunk reading a comic book. Maggie didn't seem to be aware that Crystal had missed the tour, but even if she had been, I'm sure she wouldn't have said anything. A booming voice is good, but it's certainly no match for ten feet of raw muscle.

40

As soon as we were all gathered together, Maggie produced a picnic basket full of sandwiches. Even though they were wrapped in cellophane, I could tell I wasn't going to like them. Some sandwiches just seem to give off bad vibes.

"THESE HAVE BEEN PREPARED BY THE LADIES IN THE DINING HALL," Maggie explained. "NORMALLY WE WILL BE EATING LUNCH INSIDE THE HALL, BUT TODAY WE'RE GOING TO STAY RIGHT HERE IN THE CABIN AND HAVE A GET-ACQUAINTED PICNIC. WON'T THAT BE FUN?"

It sounded more like a command than a question, so I nodded. Marilyn clapped her hands and squealed with delight.

"SHUT UP, POWERS. AFTER I PASS OUT THE SANDWICHES, I'VE GOT TO GO UP TO THE MAIN OFFICE FOR A FEW MINUTES. BUT BEFORE I LEAVE, I WANT TO GET THINGS STARTED BY HAVING ONE OF YOU INTRODUCE YOURSELF AND TELL US A LITTLE BIT ABOUT YOUR BACKGROUND. WHO WOULD LIKE TO GO FIRST?"

When no one raised her hand, Maggie smiled deviously and looked at Marilyn. "GOOD. THAT MEANS *I* GET TO CHOOSE. HOW ABOUT YOU, POWERS? YOU'RE ALWAYS SUCH A FUNNY GUY. WHY DON'T YOU BEGIN?"

I thought Marilyn got out of the situation rather

well. She grabbed the first sandwich she saw, stuffed it into her mouth, and garbled something about not being allowed to talk with her mouth full.

Disgusted, Maggie headed for the door. "POWERS, I DON'T CARE *WHO* YOUR GRANDFATHER IS. YOU'RE A GROSS PIG."

As soon as she was out of the door, Marilyn finished choking down her sandwich and smiled. "Don't worry about ol' Maggot Blocker," she explained. "I had her as a counselor last year. Her bark's a lot worse than her bite. Besides, the counselors aren't allowed to hit you or anything. The worst they can do to you is call your parents to come get you. And they only do that if it's really bad."

Crystal frowned. "Like what's really bad?"

Marilyn smiled. "A couple of years ago this girl went sort of crazy and kept ambushing people in the forest and tying them to trees. They made the girl leave, but her parents were so mad about having to fly home from the Bahamas to get her, they sued my grandfather for half a million bucks. They said that running around unsupervised had turned her into a *hooligan* . . . whatever that is."

"What happened?" I asked curiously.

"Nothing. When the suit finally got to court, the judge said he was old, and he wasn't going to spend what time he had left listening to a stupid lawsuit like that. Then he told the crazy girl's parents they were an embarrassment to the American justice system."

Crystal stood up. "Well, if they're not going to do

42

anything to me, then I'm not going to hang around here eatin' a lousy sandwich. No offense, you guys, but most of my friends are in cabin thirteen." She stomped out of the room and slammed the door behind her.

After a few seconds of silence Marilyn spoke first. "She looks so familiar to me . . . does Big Foot have a daughter?" I was the only one who laughed.

Cassandra stood up and deposited her sandwich in the trash can. "I'm not going to like it here. I can tell already. I still don't believe Pop did this to me." Putting her hands on her hips, she looked around at the rest of us. "Why did you guys come, anyway? Same reason?"

"I already told you my story," replied Marilyn. "Every July two hired thugs drag me out of my house and strap me to a bus seat, and I end up here for two weeks. Nothing I can do. And besides, my grandfather thinks I love this place. How can you tell a happy little bald guy that his camp's an armpit? Like I said before, I'm stuck."

Suddenly all eyes were on me. If anyone suspected I had actually wanted to come, I would have died. If there is one thing I've learned from my sister's popularity, it's that sometimes part of being accepted is going along with the crowd.

So now it was my turn to blame someone for putting me there. Panicking, I did the only thing that came naturally, and blamed it on . . .

"Deena!" I blurted nervously. "Er . . . Deena is my sister. She signed me up for this place as a practical joke," I explained, making it up as I went along. "When I started getting all these brochures in the mail, my parents sent in the money."

"Without even asking you?" quizzed Cassandra.

"Ah . . . yeah . . . I guess they thought it'd be a nice surprise or something," I lied. "You know how parents are."

Cass let out a groan. "What's wrong with adults these days, anyway? What's the big deal about camp all of a sudden? You show them a couple of pine trees, and the next thing you know, they're sewing your name in your underwear and shoving you out the door with a sleeping bag under your arm. You wouldn't believe the number of times my father talked about all the fresh air I'd get to breath!"

Marilyn began to chuckle. "It's a cinch your old man's never gotten a whiff of the bathrooms around here. Even the *animals* are offended."

The three of us started laughing. Fern looked like she was almost attempting to smile.

"What about you?" Marilyn asked her. "Why did you come?"

Marilyn's question caught Fern completely off guard. From the look on her face, I thought she was going to have a stroke. She sat there and gasped for at least a minute, then pulled out her canteen and began to guzzle.

Marilyn waited patiently for her to finish. She even listened to Fern suck air for a while.

"Well?" she asked at last. "What's your reason?"

This time it seemed like Fern was going to force herself to speak. But I could tell by the frantic look on her face that she was real uncomfortable about it. It was the kind of look people have when they're giving a speech in English and forget what comes after the opening sentence. Wanda calls it the F look, because that's what they usually end up getting.

Anyway, when she finally opened her mouth, she pointed at me and said, "Same as her."

Marilyn looked amazed. "Are you kidding? Your sister set it up? Is her name Deena too?"

"I've got a cousin named Nina," chimed Cassandra.

Marilyn thought for a second. "Talk about coincidences—my mother's middle name is Tina."

Things were getting out of hand.

"Er . . . I, ah, think what she means is someone signed her up without her knowing about it. Like her mother . . . or Hubby, maybe."

"Hubby?"

"Ah . . . I mean her stepfather."

"Oh. Well, why didn't she just say so?"

Fern sat there acting as though she hadn't heard the question.

Cassandra looked at me a minute and then raised her perfectly groomed eyebrows. "Are you two friends?"

"NO!" I answered much too forcefully. "I mean, no. We're not. I don't know Fern from the man in the moon, do I, Fern?"

Fern looked at me sadly.

"What I mean is, I don't know her *well*. But I do

45

know her, don't I, Fern? Not well . . . but we did meet at the bus stop, didn't we?"

Fern's eyes brightened up a little. I didn't want to hurt her. I honestly didn't. I really felt trapped in the middle.

Cass sighed. "Well, at least it's nice to know that we all feel the same way about this scum hole. No offense, Marilyn."

"Are you kidding?" Marilyn replied enthusiastically. "This is great. Last year I got stuck with a cabin full of girls who bought matching backpacks and went around singing camp songs. Believe me, there's nothing worse than waking up each morning to seven little singing weirdos. My respect for Snow White went up a ton."

"Maybe it won't be so bad after all," mused Cassandra. "Not as long as we have each other, anyway. What's that old saying? One for all and all for one?"

Marilyn saluted. "The Three Musketeers. What a great team *they* were. Not to mention a humdinger of a candy bar."

Cass laughed. "Yeah. That's us. The Three Musketeers."

Across from me, Fern turned her head quickly away . . . but not before I saw the dejection in her face. I'd have given anything not to have seen her, but I had.

Reluctantly, I cleared my throat. "Ah, don't you mean four musketeers? There're four."

Cassandra and Marilyn looked at Fern a second and then exchanged quick glances.

"Ah . . . yeah, sure," replied Marilyn at last. "Four."

46

«5»

Cass sat at the lunch table slowly shaking her head. It was the third day of camp, and she was looking very grim. "That girl is driving me up a wall," she said.

She was talking about Fern, of course. Fern had been assigned to clean up the lunch dishes, leaving the three of us alone for the first time since Saturday. Much to Cass's distress, I had promised we would wait for her.

"Cass is right," agreed Marilyn. "Look, Dinah . . . I don't mind weirdos hanging around me once in a while as long as they don't touch me or anything. But Fern Wadley is just not normal."

"She's normal," I argued weakly. "I know she may be a little dull, but . . ."

"A little dull?" interrupted Marilyn. "A *little* dull? My grandfather has a mole on his back that's more interesting than she is."

Cassandra made a face. "Please, Marilyn. I just finished eating."

"I don't care. It's true. The girl is fresh out of the

47

Twilight Zone. Have you ever noticed how she stands around sometimes and lets her tongue hang out?"

"I think she's got a postnasal drip," added Cassandra. "What's that terrible noise she makes at night? It sounds like she's clearing out her nostrils or something."

This time Marilyn was the one making the face. "Don't say *nostril*. I hate that word."

"Well, whatever she does, it's disgusting. And to make matters worse, she never lets us out of her sight for a minute. It's embarrassing to be seen with her. She's always peeking at you through that stringy hair. We've got to do something! The other night in the bathroom, I caught her looking under my door to make sure my feet were still there. She didn't even act embarrassed. She just got up off the floor, brushed off her knees, and followed me back to the cabin."

Marilyn groaned. "The trouble is, she doesn't even *try* to act normal. Remember yesterday when we were talking about TV and Dinah asked her who her favorite comedians were?"

Cassandra nodded. "Who could forget it? She said, 'Heckle and Jeckle.'"

I put my head down on the table and covered it up with my arms. Everything they were saying was true. Instead of coming out of her shell, Fern was getting harder and harder to live with. She followed us around camp like a lost puppy. She rarely spoke, and when she did, it was usually to apologize for bumping into our backs or stepping on our feet. In a mere three days she had already pulled my shoes off my heels seven times.

Next to my seventh-grade social studies teacher, Fern Wadley was the most uninteresting person I had ever met in my life. It was like trying to be friends with a bowl of Cream of Wheat. She never got enthused over anything or laughed and giggled like the rest of us. She didn't talk about boys. I asked her once if she had a boyfriend, and she didn't answer for so long that I changed the subject.

I guess you might think that someone so quiet wouldn't be much of a bother, but in addition to being boring, Fern also had a few personal habits that made me sick. Each night before she went to bed, she did something with her feet. Sometimes it looked like she was picking off dead skin. Other times she would just rub them. Once she asked me for a barrette and used the end of it to clean her toenails. If I had known, I never would have lent it to her. She started to give it back, but I told her to keep it. Just thinking about putting it back in my hair made me queasy.

I didn't like Fern any better after three days than I did when we first met. But unfortunately, no matter how much she picked her feet, I just couldn't bring myself to do anything that might hurt her. Thinking of yourself as "The Kind One" is a hard habit to break.

Peeking out from the opening in my arms, I sighed. "Maybe once she gets to know us better, she won't be so bad. Maybe she's only letting her tongue flop around because she can't think of enough stuff to say to us yet. Maybe . . ."

49

Cassandra held up a hand for me to stop. "Maybe we'd better just get rid of her," she said quietly.

Marilyn nodded her approval. "Face it, Dinah. The girl has *got* to go."

"I guess so," I said hesitantly. I had known that was what they were going to say, but that didn't make thinking about it any easier. "But where is she supposed to go?"

"Anywhere we're not," said Marilyn breezily, getting up from the table.

Cass stood up too and gave me a pat on the shoulder. "Don't worry about it. Marilyn and I have a lot of faith in you. We know you'll think of something. And believe me, you'll feel a whole lot better about it if you take care of it right now. We'll meet you at the lake for our two o'clock swim."

The two of them were almost out of the dining-hall door before what she had said really hit me.

"OH, NO YOU DON'T!" I shouted, chasing after them. "YOU CAN'T JUST LEAVE ME LIKE THIS. YOU CAN'T! I MEAN *I* CAN'T! I MEAN . . ."

Cass waited for me to catch up. "Listen, Dinah. I want to be honest with you. I like you. I really do. But the fact of the matter is, *you're* the one responsible for Fern being in our cabin, not Marilyn or me. And therefore, I think you should be kind enough to dump her."

Kind enough to dump her, I repeated to myself. Kind enough to dump her. Something about it sounded strange, but I couldn't quite put my finger on it. There was certainly nothing wrong with the part about being kind. . . .

"I think it's the dumping part I'm not crazy about," I concluded at last. "I've got to be honest with you guys—I'm what you'd call a sucker. I have this *thing* about hurting people's feelings."

Cassandra put her hands on her hips. "Don't tell me that you've never told anyone to get lost before."

I shrugged. "My sister. But she expects it. It's the foundation of our relationship."

"Well, maybe *dumping* was a poor choice of words," she said. "Why don't we call it something else? Why don't we just say you'll be giving her the opportunity to make new friends? But no matter what we call it, I'm telling you, Dinah, getting rid of Fern Wadley is probably one of the nicest things you can do for her."

Marilyn raised her eyebrows. "This ought to be a good one."

"No. I *mean* it," continued Cass. "Just think about it for a minute. By getting Fern out on her own, you'll be giving her a chance to try and find someone with whom she has something in common. You know . . . someone else who's backward and gross. Believe me, Fern Wadley isn't the only camper I've seen around here who lets you look inside her mouth when she chews. Just think how much happier she'd be if she could pal around with someone more her own style. Maybe she could finally relax and get her nasals to stop dripping."

Marilyn looked impressed. "I've got to admit, that came out better than I expected. When you think about it, it makes a lot of sense. Having Fern hang around with us only points out how much of a nerd she is. If you match her up with another nerd, they'll sort of cancel each other out. It's like two negatives makes a positive. It's nature's way."

Cass clapped her hands delightedly. "Of course it is. We're not trying to be mean, Dinah. We just think that Fern would have a much better time if she found someone she could be more *comfortable* with."

I thought it over and sighed. Maybe they were right. It really did make sense. Fern was sort of like one of Nana's sweaters. If you put her on with fancy designer clothes, she'd stick out like a sore thumb. But if you tucked her into a faded pair of Nana's old polyester pants, she'd probably be a lot more at home. And that's what Ilsa and Hubby wanted, didn't they? For Fern to feel comfortable enough to come out of her shell?

"Yeah . . . well, okay. I guess I just never thought of it like that. Opportunity to make new friends, huh?"

"Right. Exactly!" squealed Cassandra. "She'll thank you for it. You'll see."

"Ah . . . there's just one more thing," I added hesitantly.

"What's that?"

I took a deep breath. "I don't suppose either one of you would like to give Fern the good news, would you? I'm just not sure I can stand to see all the happiness in her face when she finds out she's being dumped."

52

Marilyn threw her hands in the air in frustration. "Oh, okay," she snapped. "If you're going to make such a big deal about it, I'll do the dumping. I've probably had more experience at it, anyway. When your grandfather owns a camp, there are always a bunch of bozos following you that you can't stand. You wouldn't *believe* the things they try to bribe me with. One boy actually brought me a cherry fruit pie every day for two weeks."

"What happened?"

Marilyn grinned. "When I finally got sick of cherry pies and told him it was a *girls'* camp, he punched me in the back and stepped on my sandwich."

I laughed and patted her on the arm. "I really appreciate you doing this for me. I just don't think I'd be good at it."

"I probably would," offered Cass. "But I read somewhere that confrontation can make your skin break out."

Marilyn rolled her eyes. "There's not going to *be* a confrontation, Cassandra. I'm very good at this. Dumping someone is like pulling off a Band-Aid; the slower you do it, the more it hurts. That's why I came up with a standard speech. It's clever, yet quick and painless. It goes like this: 'We don't like you.'"

Cass and I stood there a minute and stared at each other. I didn't know whether to laugh or cry.

"'We don't like you.' That's it?" I asked finally.

Cassandra shook her head. "No offense, Marilyn, but 'We don't like you' isn't really that great. I mean, I want to get rid of the girl and everything, but I don't want her slobbering into her pillow all night long. She makes enough disgusting noises as it is. Couldn't you just tell her that we took a vote and decided that she would be happier if she found a nice little dullard to pal around with? You know, make it sound democratic. Who can argue with democracy?"

"Dullard?" repeated Marilyn.

Cass shrugged nonchalantly. "It's the adult word for nerd."

Suddenly I stopped feeling relieved. Even though they had convinced me that Fern would have to go, I couldn't help thinking that we should at least try to be as nice about it as we could. And let's face it . . . no matter how you say it, "We don't like you" has a bit of a bite to it. I guess you could say I've always believed in pulling my Band-Aids off a little more slowly. If I wanted it done right, I'd have to do it myself.

"Wait!" I blurted. "I've changed my mind. You're right. I'm the reason Fern's in the cabin, so I should be the one to handle this. You two go on ahead, and I'll go back to the kitchen and talk to her."

Cassandra broke into a huge smile. "I *knew* you wouldn't let us down. And just remember, even though Marilyn and I aren't with you, you have our total support. Doesn't she, Marilyn?"

"Total," agreed Marilyn. "And don't worry. If she doesn't take the news well, you can always hire Crystal as a bodyguard."

"Bodyguard?"

54

Marilyn started to laugh. "Yeah. You never know about dullards. Sometimes they sneak out in the middle of the night and try to get'cha."

Some support.

I turned to go back to the kitchen, but Fern was just coming out the door. She was still a little frazzled from her cleanup duties. Her upper lip was sweaty, and there was a small piece of lettuce stuck to her cheek. As soon as she saw me, she immediately began looking around for Cass and Marilyn.

"Ah, they're not here," I began explaining nervously. "Cass and Marilyn, that is. They decided not to wait."

Staring her usual stare, Fern walked beside me as I talked. After a few steps she opened her mouth and began scraping her teeth with her fingernails. I tried not to look and instead concentrated on what I had to say.

"You see, the thing is, Fern, I'm afraid that with four of us going around together all the time, things are getting sort of crowded. Well, not crowded exactly . . . just sort of awkward, I mean. I think it's the number four that's doing it, Fern. Four really isn't a very good number for friendships. I mean, when you think about it, almost all famous friendships are made up of threes. Let's see . . . you've got the Three Stooges, and the Three Blind Mice. And then there's Huey, Dewey, and Louie; the Pep Boys—Manny, Mo, and Jack; and of course, as Marilyn mentioned the other day, the world-famous Three Musketeers."

I waited a second to see if Fern wanted to say anything, but all she did was burp. It was a quiet burp, but I still heard it.

"Another big lunch, eh, Fern?"

She nodded.

"Well, speaking of big lunches, I bet the Three Musketeers ate big lunches. There *were* only three of them, though, Fern. Not four, like I said on Saturday. I wish there *had* been four of them. But let's face it, the Three Musketeers are pretty deeply rooted in history, and I really don't think that a bunch of kids at camp ought to tamper with something like that, do you? Heh, heh. I mean, old Alexander Dumas might not like it if we added another musketeer to his book. Er . . . Alexander Dumas . . . he's the one who wrote it. French guy, I think."

Fern frowned as if she were giving the matter some thought.

"Anyway, you know what *I* think would be good, Fern? I think it would be a great experience for you if you tried to assert yourself a little bit and get out and meet someone new. Wouldn't your mother be proud if you did something like that? Like maybe in swimming class this afternoon, you could walk right up to someone you think you might like and say, 'Hi there. Would you like to be my buddy today?' Just think how great you'd feel if you did something bold like that!"

Cautiously, I looked over to see her reaction. Much to my surprise, a small sheepish grin was making its way across her face.

"Well," I continued, encouraged, "do you think you could say something like that, Fern?"

She nodded shyly and then suddenly took a deep breath and closed her eyes. "Do you think you could be my buddy today?" she repeated in a voice barely above a whisper.

"Good! That was perfect!" I squealed, patting her arm in approval. "See? There's nothing to it. That's all it takes. Just pick out someone who looks nice, and before you know it, you'll have all *kinds* of buddies around here. You'll see. Well, keep me posted, okay? I've got to go meet Cass and Marilyn at the lake. Maybe I'll see you down there."

Fern didn't seem to be listening. Instead, she closed her eyes again. "Do you think you could be my buddy today?" she repeated.

"Ah . . . yeah . . . like I said, Fern, that's good, very good. You just keep practicing and maybe I'll see you down at the—"

"No. *You*, Dinah! Do you think *you* could be my buddy today?"

For a second I stood perfectly rigid as my brain panicked. I tried to order my feet to run, but they insisted on standing there as stupidly as the rest of me. Soon I became aware of a sick feeling building in the pit of my stomach. I recognized it immediately. It's called doom. It's the same feeling you get when your mother finds out the "PG" movie you told her you were going to see was really an "R."

I was trapped. Trapped, and doomed with unco-operative feet.

Fern fidgeted nervously as she waited for my answer. Her eyes were full of hope, and her mouth twitched and smiled at the same time.

No! I screamed silently. I *won't* be your buddy. I *can't!* It's them or you, Fern. And I choose them!

But deep inside I knew there was no way in the world I would ever get those words to come out of my mouth. And that's what made me doomed. Doomed to the company of a burping girl with lettuce stuck to her cheek.

There was nothing left to do but accept defeat. As my father once said, "When you're caught, you're caught. Trying to wiggle out of a trap only makes it tighter and more uncomfortable." At the time he was talking to a mouse he had caught, but it still applied.

In a last desperate move, I looked all around me for help. I don't know who I expected to save me, but who-ever it was didn't show up. There was only Fern, stand-ing there waiting for an answer. And finally, I had no choice.

"Yeah, sure, Fern." I sighed. "I'll be your buddy."

I'd like to put the rest of the afternoon out of my mind forever. It was bad enough that Fern showed up at the lake wearing a nose plug and goggles. But when she took her test and I found out she couldn't swim, I thought I'd die. The counselor made me tow her around while she kicked her feet.

Marilyn made a series of loud tugboat noises as I navigated Fern around the shallow water. Finally she started laughing so hard, she had to be pulled out of the water by a lifeguard. Cassandra simply pretended not to know me.

Later that night, after Fern was asleep, I explained to Cass and Marilyn what had happened. I could tell they both felt a little sorry for me. Marilyn apologized for laughing and said that it sounded like Fern was going to be a tough nut to crack.

Cassandra gave me a reassuring smile. "Don't worry, Dinah. It'll all work out. You'll think of something."

But unfortunately I didn't. And two more days passed with Fern still hot on our trail. I could tell that Cass and Marilyn were losing their patience. Especially Cass. She didn't say much, but I still knew. Every time she looked at me, the message in her eyes was clear. "For Pete's sake, Dinah," they seemed to say, "when in the world are you going to dump her?" In a way it was amusing. Cass did more talking with her eyes than Fern did with her mouth.

As usual, Marilyn wasn't quite as quiet when it came to expressing her feelings. On Wednesday night the counselors showed a movie in the dining hall. After the four of us were seated on the floor, Marilyn turned abruptly and asked Fern to kindly stop breathing down her neck. Fern complied and switched to *my* neck.

"I'm going to tell her," I explained later that evening when Fern surprised us all by taking her first solo trip to the bathroom. "I promise. It's just that I'm having a hard time finding the right moment to hit her with it."

"Well, you'd better hurry up, or you're going to run out of time," said Marilyn. "I've got something planned for the end of the week, but it's only for the three of us."

Cass raised her eyebrows. "What is it? Is it a surprise?"

"You'll see," replied Marilyn slyly. "Right now we've got to work on Dinah to give Fern the word."

"I know. I know," I said defensively. "I was going to do it yesterday in arts and crafts. I had it all planned. I was going to tell her while she was busy working so she wouldn't have a lot of time to dwell on it."

Cass put her hands on her hips. "Well, why didn't you?"

I sighed. "I don't know. When I saw how frustrated she was getting with her project, I just couldn't bring myself to do it."

Cass rolled her eyes. "It's an ugly ceramic beaver, for heaven's sake. How nice can she expect it to be?"

"True. But Dinah's got a point. Even for an ugly ceramic beaver, it's ugly," added Marilyn. "Have you seen the mouth she painted on that poor guy? It takes up half his head. He looks like he ran face first into a logjam."

Cassandra wasn't amused. "It's no worse than most of the other projects around here. *No one* seems to have any taste. Half the camp's making ceramic animals, and the rest of them are making those tacky braided necklaces."

"Lanyards," corrected Marilyn. "But they're not really necklaces. They're supposed to hold whistles."

"Well, whatever they're supposed to do, they're ugly. Today I saw one that was pea green and red. Think about it. Who'd ever be caught dead wearing a pea green and red lanyard?"

Marilyn frowned as she gave the matter some thought. "How about Santa?"

Cassandra shook her head firmly. "No," she said. "Hunter green, maybe, or forest green. But never pea green. And besides, who wants a whistle attached to their neck? Name one person you know, besides Maggie Blocker, who goes around blowing a whistle."

Marilyn managed to keep a straight face. "I've gotta go with Santa again," she replied seriously. "Those darned little elves can get pretty rowdy."

"Well, I don't care *who* wears them," retorted Cass. "I still think the project we chose is the only one with any class. The macramé belts we're making are going to look so cute with jeans and a couple of polos, don't you think?"

I nodded, but Marilyn only shrugged. Marilyn wasn't really into clothes any more than *I* was. She didn't wear hand-me-downs or anything, but most of her shirts were the kind with sayings on the front. Some were serious, like her SAVE THE WHALES shirt. Others she had designed herself, like the one that said RAYMOND FLINKER'S A DRIP. He's the kid who stepped on her sandwich.

Even so, in the end she had agreed to make a macramé belt. She said that in eight years of camp, she had already made more lanyards than you could wear in a lifetime. "Thanks to my mother, lanyards are one thing that the needy no longer need," she explained. "If you ever hear a bum blowing a whistle, chances are he's got one of my lanyards around his neck. Just once, I'd like to make a project that the Salvation Army doesn't haul away at Christmas."

Cass was wrong when she said that most of the other girls were making lanyards and animals. They only started out making stuff like that. A lot of them switched when they saw how cute her belt was turning out. Things like that happen when you're the Cassandra Barnhill type. You end up influencing people you don't even know. I think it's called swaying the masses.

I'm still amazed at how much attention she attracted. With Cass, it was almost impossible to go anywhere in camp without having at least one total stranger ask her where she bought her clothes.

Once I had a stranger ask me where I bought an outfit. It was last Halloween. I was wearing my ketchup bottle.

But like I said before, Cassandra was different. She attracted people whether she wanted to or not. When you looked at her you got the feeling that someday she was going to be a Miss Something-or-other, like America or Universe. Well, maybe not America or Universe, but at least a city or county. Her name alone would win it for her. Beauty queens are almost never named anything ordinary, like Helen or Betty . . . or

Dinah. Also, her middle name was Leigh. Mine is Frieda.

Cassandra Leigh Barnhill wasn't the only one in our cabin who was becoming well known. Marilyn Powers was running a close second. She wasn't the beauty queen type, but she was definitely funny. And sometimes, being funny is just as good as being beautiful. Maybe even better.

Besides, as soon as the news spread that her grandfather owned the place, we hardly ever ate a meal without someone pointing at our table. It was really exciting. I'd been pointed at before, of course, but only because something was unbuttoned. This was a different kind of pointing—a good kind. And I'd be lying if I didn't admit that it was even better than I thought it would be.

Suddenly I could see Fern in the distance, making her way back from the bathroom. Cass saw her, too, and put an arm around my shoulder.

"Listen, Dinah," she said quietly. "I know it seems like I'm always trying to pressure you about this, but the truth is, the better Fern knows us, the worse she gets. Today at lunch, when she was eating her alphabet soup, she made the word *poo* on her spoon and put it in my bowl."

I couldn't help but laugh. "It was supposed to be *boo*. She did the same thing to me. Your *b* probably got turned around."

"*Boo, poo*, what difference does it make? The point is, she—"

Just then the door slammed, and Fern came shuffling into the cabin. She was wearing her red-and-white polka-dot pajamas and there was toothpaste drool on her chin. I know you shouldn't dislike someone just because of a little toothpaste drool. I mean, that's what they try to teach you in church. But in church it's easier. No one's sitting there with toothpaste drool running down their face.

I watched out of the corner of my eye as Fern crawled into her bunk and zipped her sleeping bag up around her. Then I sighed. Cassandra was right. I really had to do something.

"Tomorrow," I whispered. "I promise. I'll tell her tomorrow."

«6»

On Thursday morning, by the time I heard Maggie's wake-up whistle, Crystal was already dressed and on her way out the door.

"HOLD IT! HOLD IT RIGHT THERE, BALL," bellowed Maggie. "I HAVE AN ANNOUNCE-MENT TO MAKE!"

"So do I," snapped Crystal. "Don't call me Ball."

"THE ANNOUNCEMENT IS AS FOLLOWS," continued Maggie. "TOMORROW NIGHT THERE WILL BE A TALENT CONTEST. EACH CABIN IS URGED TO HAVE AT LEAST ONE ENTRY. WE WILL COMPETE AGAINST THE OTHER CABINS FOR TROPHIES AND OTHER PRIZES.

"FOR THOSE OF YOU WHO SING OR DANCE, THERE WILL BE A PIANO PLAYER IN THE RECREATION ROOM FOR THE NEXT TWO DAYS TO HELP WITH YOUR MUSIC. THERE ARE ALSO A NUMBER OF RECORDS AVAILABLE ON A FIRST COME, FIRST SERVED BASIS.

"YOU MAY ENTER THE COMPETITION EITHER AS A GROUP OR INDIVIDUALLY, BUT EITHER WAY, YOU WILL REPRESENT CABIN ELEVEN. I'M SURE THAT I CAN COUNT ON ALL FIVE OF YOU TO COME UP WITH A TASTEFUL PERFORMANCE." Maggie stopped and looked at Marilyn. "CORRECTION. MAKE THAT FOUR OF YOU," she said sarcastically. "I FORGOT ABOUT POWERS."

"No. Make that three of you," interjected Crystal, who had started for the door again. "I don't go in for stuff like that. I never know what to do."

Behind me, Marilyn cleared her throat. "Perhaps you could wrestle Godzilla," she suggested somewhat timidly.

We all breathed a lot easier when Crystal laughed. "Nah," she replied, waving her hand as the screen door closed behind her. "I'll leave the song-and-dance crap up to the rest of you guys."

Marilyn watched her go. "Song-and-dance crap," she repeated. "You've got to admit, the big fella really has a way with words."

For the next few minutes Maggie continued to give us more details about the upcoming contest: how long each performance could last, who the judges would be . . . things like that. But the whole time she was talking, Marilyn was in the back of the cabin, busily rummaging through her duffel bag.

After Maggie had stopped shouting and we had begun to get our clothes on, Marilyn caught my eye and secretly motioned me over. As I approached she put her finger to her lips.

"Don't say anything. Just listen. I was hoping you would have our little problem with you-know-who taken care of by now. But since you don't, I'm going to have to let you in on my secret."

"What se—?"

"Shh!" she ordered. "Not so loud! It's the surprise I told you about a couple of days ago. Remember?"

This time I just nodded.

Checking to make sure Fern wasn't looking, Marilyn tilted her duffel bag in my direction. "It's in here," she mouthed silently. "Look."

She opened the top of the bag wide enough for me to look inside, but it was dark and hard to see. I tried to pull the bag open wider, and my hand touched something smooth and soft and—

"Furry!" I gasped.

Immediately, everyone in the cabin turned to look. Panicking, Marilyn jumped in front of the duffel bag.

"Heh, heh, heh . . . ah, don't mind us, folks. We were thinking about maybe writing a poem for the talent show, weren't we, Dinah? . . . and, ah . . . we need to come up with something that rhymes with *furry*. Ah, let's see now . . . there's flurry, blurry . . . worry . . ."

"Hurry," offered Cass.

Marilyn snapped her fingers. "Good one! Hurry. We'll use it. Well . . . thanks a lot."

We got some funny looks, but finally the others went back to dressing.

"I *told* you to be quiet!" hissed Marilyn.

"I'm sorry," I whispered. "It's just that I was so shocked! *Please*, Marilyn, tell me you haven't brought some kind of dead animal in here. I've got this old dog at home, see, and I just don't think I could . . ."

Marilyn didn't let me finish. "Yeah. Right," she said disgustedly. "It's part of my Bring a Dead Cat to Camp campaign. Get serious, will you?"

"Okay, okay. Sorry," I murmured, trying to settle her down. But what was I supposed to think? "It *is* furry, isn't it? If it's not a dead animal, what is it?"

Marilyn's eyes lit up. "It's costumes! Costumes for the talent show. *Three* of them. Get it? *Three.*" Unfortunately, Marilyn's enthusiasm had caused her voice to become louder than a whisper.

"Get what?" called Cassandra as she eagerly sprinted over to us. Fern was right on her heels. "Did you say something about costumes?"

"Er . . . ah," stuttered Marilyn, trying to wink at Cass and close her duffel bag at the same time. "Yeah. They're for the contest. I'll show you later."

Getting the hint, Cass winked back and retreated. Fern continued to crane her neck as she tried to peer into the bag.

"I *said* I'll show you later, Fern!" Marilyn repeated sternly.

Reluctantly, Fern plodded back to her bunk to finish dressing. As soon as she was out of hearing range, Marilyn nudged me.

"They're *cannibal* costumes," she mouthed, point-

68

ing to her bag. "We're going to be cannibals. It's that fake fur stuff. But there are only three of them. Understand? Three costumes, four girls? No room for Fern. Don't you see, Dinah? It's the perfect excuse to give her the news without taking any of the blame." Marilyn smiled at her own cleverness. "Don't bother to thank me now. You can do the explaining while Cass and I go to breakfast. Meet you there in about twenty minutes."

I was still in a state of confusion when she grabbed Cassandra's arm and headed out the cabin door. Cass was as surprised as I was. She only had enough time to put on one polo.

As the screen door began to close, Marilyn smiled. "You can do it, kiddo," she said out loud. "See you in twenty."

Still trying to sort out my feelings, I stood silently and watched them go. This was it, I thought. They had been patient letting Fern tag around with us all week, but I couldn't put it off any longer. It was time for me to do what I had promised. And besides, Marilyn was right. It was a perfect opportunity. After all, it certainly wasn't my fault that she had only brought three costumes. It wasn't anyone's fault. It was fate. There was nothing to feel guilty about.

It wasn't like I was waiting until the last minute. Fern would still have two days to come up with a talent presentation of her own. Maybe she could do a demonstration of something—toenail cleaning, perhaps. . . .

I was still deep in thought when I felt a sharp tap on

my shoulder. I rolled my eyes. Fern was probably playing another joke. When I turned around, I was sure she would pretend she hadn't done it. Ever since I had been her swimming buddy, she had been doing stuff like that more and more.

Don't ask me why, but I turned around anyway.

"How 'bout *dirty?*" she said, grinning stupidly.

"Er . . . excuse me?"

"*Dirty.* You know, to rhyme with *furry.*"

Unfortunately, I knew Fern well enough to be certain this was no joke.

"Ah . . . yeah, sure, Fern. Dirty . . . furry. We'll keep it in mind."

I heard her stomach begin to growl. She doubled in half to keep the noise down.

"Wanna go eat, buddy?" she muttered.

That was another problem. She had started calling me buddy.

I took a deep breath. It was now or never.

"Yeah. Okay, Fern," I replied as I opened the cabin door for her. "But first there's something I really need to talk to you about. . . ."

Ten minutes later I walked into the dining hall. Cassandra and Marilyn were already eating. I could tell they were surprised to see me so soon. They were even more surprised to see Fern still by my side.

I grinned sheepishly. No one grinned back. Instead, their eyes demanded an explanation.

"Well . . . ah . . . we're in luck," I sputtered, trying not to look at them.

"Luck?" questioned Marilyn.

"Yeah. Ah . . . well, it's just like we thought. Good old Fern, here, has agreed to be in our pot."

Marilyn raised her eyebrows. "Our what?"

"Er . . . our pot. You know. Cannibals always have a pot, don't they? The, ah, cannibal cooking pot."

Marilyn stared blankly for a moment and then turned to Cassandra. "The cannibal cooking pot," she repeated in disbelief. "Good old Fern has agreed to be in our cannibal cooking pot." Then she slowly lowered her head to the table and began banging it gently against the edge.

After a moment Cass took charge and pulled her up. "Let me get this straight," she said. "You mean the three of us are going to be cannibals, and Fern will be sitting in our pot?"

Fern giggled. "You can stir me," she replied. The thought of it made her giggle even harder. It sounded like it was coming out of the mouth of Porky Pig. Marilyn lowered her head and began banging again.

Cass tried to remain calm. "Are you *sure* you want to be in the pot, Fern?" she asked. "I mean, are you positive you wouldn't be happier doing an act on your own? Don't you play the kazoo or something?"

Fern thought a moment, then, apparently deciding it was a joke, giggled even harder.

Cassandra couldn't take it anymore and chose to

71

leave the table. A minute later Marilyn said she was getting a headache and excused herself to go take an aspirin.

Things were beginning to backfire, and I knew it. It was clear that by not getting rid of Fern, I was driving Cass and Marilyn away from me. But I just couldn't help what had happened. I had tried to tell Fern about the costumes, I really had. But when I got to the part about there only being three of them, she had interrupted me before I had a chance to finish.

"You don't want me in your skit, do you?" she had muttered quietly. And as soon as the words were out of her mouth, I'd known there was no way in the world I could answer truthfully. What was I supposed to say: No, we can't stand you?

Maybe Marilyn could have said it, and maybe Cass could, but that kind of truth was just too hard for me. That's why I came up with the pot idea. And if that made me a liar, I guess I was a liar. . . .

More than anything, though, it made me mad. Mad that I had to be in this situation in the first place. Mad that Fern couldn't even *try* to act normal. Surely she knew what normal was. She had a television, didn't she? Did anyone on television go around scraping their teeth with their fingernails or letting their tongues hang out? It wasn't like she couldn't help herself. She was gross, not stupid.

And anyway, even if she didn't have a television, she had eyes. Couldn't she see she didn't fit in and would be better off finding her own kind of friend? My dog

Rollo's not normal either, but he doesn't hang out at AKC dog shows trying to pal around with the winners.

Why, I asked myself, did I keep letting Fern's feelings come before mine? Why were mine always second? How much did I really owe Fern Wadley, anyway? Was it more than I owed myself? After a lifetime of black hockey skates and hand-me-downs, didn't I deserve a chance to be on top for a change? Just this once?

I sighed and watched Cassandra and Marilyn leave the dining hall. Across from me, Fern was shoveling in eggs and washing them down with tomato juice. When she finally put the glass down, she was wearing a red mustache. A couple of girls at the next table pointed at us. This time it wasn't the good kind.

I put my head in my hands. Maybe I had gone too far with this "kindness" business. Maybe I was trying to be *too* kind. That's why I was having so much trouble.

I took a closer look at the girl I was trying to protect. Fern smiled shyly. There was egg on her tooth. It wasn't much. But it was all I needed to come to a decision.

After the talent show I would stand up for myself. I would ask Fern to make a few new friends, and that was that. It didn't have to sound mean. I'd be pleasant but firm. After all, there would still be a week left for her to meet someone new. I had taken care of her the first week; she could certainly take care of herself for the second one. Fifty-fifty. That was fair, wasn't it? A week for her, a week for me. What could be fairer than fifty-fifty?

Feeling a little more in control of things, I handed Fern a napkin. If I was going to be firm, I might as well get started. "You've got egg on your tooth," I said boldly.

She giggled like Porky Pig again and wiped it off. Then the two of us walked back to the cabin.

« 7 »

Cass and Marilyn calmed down faster than I had expected. I have a feeling that trying on the costumes had something to do with it. Cass said her mother once told her that beautiful women and furs belonged together, even if both were phonies.

Also, it didn't hurt that stirring someone in a pot promised to be the hit of the skit. The ladies in the kitchen found us a large old-fashioned washtub to use as a pot. The arts-and-crafts instructor let us paint it black so it would look more like a cannibal cooking pot. As soon as Fern sat down in it, Cass and Marilyn couldn't help but laugh.

Marilyn really surprised us with all the preparation she had put into the show. She said that after eight years of watching amateurs, she'd decided it was time someone brought a class act to camp. She even brought music for the piano. The costumes and the music came from one of her mother's women's club shows.

When we took the music to Jill, the piano player, she looked at it and frowned.

" 'Row, Row, Row Your Boat'? This is the song you're singing? How very original."

Marilyn winked at Cass and me. "Yeah. Well, we've changed the words around a little bit. How about if you just play the tune, and we'll do the singing?"

She handed us the sheets of words, Fern got in the pot, and we began our rehearsal, cannibal-style:

Stir, stir, stir the soup,
Taste it with a spoon,
Yummy, yummy, yummy, yummy,
Hope she'll be done soon.

Sniff, sniff, sniff the meat,
Salt it like you should,
Tasty, tasty, tasty, tasty,
Humans taste so good.

Slurp, slurp, slurp it down,
Never get enough,
Hope we trap more humans soon,
We're crazy 'bout this stuff.

Whew, phew, burp, I'm full,
Think I'm going to pop,
Phooey, phooey, phooey, phooey,
Guess I'll have to stop.

Gosh, darn, golly gee,
Wish it wasn't so,
Oh, well, what the heck,
Pass me one more toe.

By the time we were finished, the three of us were laughing so hard my stomach hurt. Jill said it was the grossest set of lyrics she had ever heard in her life. She was majoring in music, and I think the pressure of college had destroyed her sense of humor.

Anyway, when you put the song and the pot and Fern together with the furry cannibal costumes, it was obvious that we were going to have the best talent presentation in the camp. The outfits alone would have been enough to make us win. They looked like something Wilma Flintstone would wear. I doubt if cannibals really wear caveman clothes, but I liked them just the same. We even planned to chew on a few chicken bones to make it more realistic.

Fern was supposed to be a jungle explorer or something, so Marilyn told her she could just wear her own stuff. Fortunately she didn't select her Mickey Mouse getup.

I had never been in a talent contest before, and I was surprised that I wasn't nervous. I had been in a piano recital once, but that's not really the same thing. And as it turned out, I had good reason to be nervous about that one. My teacher had scheduled me to play right after Roger McCorkle. Roger was a five-year-old whose mother forced him to take lessons. He got so nervous about the recital that he wet the piano bench halfway through his performance. I know it wasn't his fault, but it did put a damper on the rest of the recital.

But the night of the talent show was different. I couldn't believe how confident I felt, knowing I was going to be in the best skit of the night with two of the most popular girls in camp.

A stage had been set up at the far end of the dining hall. As we went in, each entry in the show picked a number. We picked number twelve. It turned out to be a good selection.

The act we followed was pretty depressing. This girl from the Ever-Greenies recited a poem she had written herself about being far away from home and being eaten by a bear. It ended when she was in heaven and her parents were crying because they had sent her to camp against her will. By the time she was finished, the audience was ready for a good laugh.

I can still hear the way they giggled when Fern sat down in the pot and the three of us began to stir. And when Jill gave us our cue and we started to sing, I thought the roof was going to cave in from all the laughter. We had to sing it twice just to make sure everyone had heard it. At the end the applause was so loud, the next act had to wait about ten minutes for everyone to settle down.

It was probably one of the best things that had ever happened to me. No, it was *the* best. After the performance I hugged Marilyn and Cassandra over and over again. I even hugged Fern. Not as tightly, but a hug is a hug.

We won, of course. We each got a small trophy of our own and a Camp Miniwawa sun visor. But for me, the nicest prize was yet to come.

The next morning, as I was waiting in the breakfast

line, two little Daffy Ducklings were standing a few feet behind me, pointing. Naturally, since Cass and Marilyn were already sitting down, the first thing I did was check my buttons. When I found that everything was fastened, I was puzzled and looked back at them again.

That's when I realized that they weren't pointing at me and laughing. They were pointing at me and *admiring*. Actually admiring *me*—just me, Dinah Frieda Feeney! For the first time in my life I really felt I had made it to the top. I didn't mention it to anyone, of course. I was sure that this sort of thing happened to Cass and Marilyn all the time, so I didn't want to make a big deal out of it. But there was no denying that the top was special. And as long as I was at camp, it's where I wanted to stay.

It's too bad Fern didn't follow my example. Winning really seemed to bring out the worst in her. When we got back to the cabin that night, she put on her sun visor and started swinging me all over the cabin. "Wheeee!" she sang out. "Let's celebrate!" I tried to make her release her grip, but when someone's got you by the wrists, there's not much you can do. Since Cass and Marilyn were practically in hysterics laughing at me, Fern thought we were having fun. She didn't quit until I collapsed on the floor and refused to stand up. Even then, she went on dragging me around in a circle.

I was hoping she'd settle down after a good night's sleep. But the next morning she started right in again. Marilyn was hardly out of bed before Fern grabbed one

79

of her wrists and reached for the other one to start swinging. Marilyn slapped her hand and told her to knock it off.

Fern looked a little hurt. But by breakfast she had regained her confidence and began pinching us under the table and pretending that she hadn't. Finally Marilyn said that if she felt one more pinch, she would hire Crystal to break her fingers. Don't ask me why, but when Fern heard that, she tried to duck under the table like she was hiding. When she found there wasn't enough room, she just put her head down on her tray and covered it with her hands. You could tell she was giggling under there, but no one was sure why. When she came up again, she was still laughing. She had milk on her bangs from her cereal bowl.

Cassandra rolled her eyes and stood up. "Excuse me," she said. "But I think I've had all the fun I can stand for one morning. I'm getting out of here."

"You can't go!" blurted Fern, jumping up beside her. "We're a team now! We celebrities need to stick together!" And before Cass knew what hit her, Fern pounded her playfully on the back, so hard she knocked her right to the floor.

It was really humiliating. Cass's tray turned upside down, covering her with leftover milk, toast crusts, and orange juice. Two or three soggy cornflakes flew up and stuck in her hair.

Quickly, Fern bent down and tried to lift Cass up. "GET YOUR HANDS OFF ME, YOU LUNK-HEAD!" Cassandra screamed.

Everyone started to laugh. Kids all over the room were standing up and coming over to see what had happened.

Cass clearly wasn't used to drawing this sort of attention. She didn't try to laugh at herself or pretend to think it was funny, the way I've learned to do over the years. Instead, she just got up and rushed out the door.

Fern stood like a goof watching her go. Marilyn and I just sat there. I was in shock, but I think Marilyn was trying not to laugh.

Finally Marilyn stood up. "I'd better go find Cass," she said.

I started to get up to go with her, but Marilyn shook her head. "Maybe it would be better if I went alone this time." She glanced at Fern and back again. "That is . . . ah, if you know what I mean."

I did. It meant I was going to get stuck with Fern all day. But I didn't really have a choice.

I knew it wouldn't be a good idea to go back to the cabin right away, because Cass was there, so I decided to go for a hike in the woods to think things through. Fern came along, uninvited. I tried not to talk to her much, but she kept tripping over twigs and branches and falling into my back. Twice we knocked heads. Both times she actually said "Bonk."

By the end of the afternoon I was about to go crazy. I went to dinner as soon as the dining hall opened and was surprised to find Cass and Marilyn already there. I wasn't sure what to expect, but luckily Cass was calm. She motioned for me to sit down. I think she and

Marilyn felt a little guilty about having left me alone.

Fern slipped in next to me and, as usual, began shoveling down her food. It was obvious she had forgotten all about what had happened at breakfast.

Cassandra stared at her with disgust. "Perhaps if we pull the sides of your mouth wider, Fern, you could get the entire tray in."

Fern was smacking too loudly to hear her; but Marilyn didn't laugh, and neither did I. Nothing seemed very funny anymore.

«8»

My mother calls it reaching the end of her rope. My father just points to his neck and says he's had it up to here. There are probably a lot more expressions for the way I felt, but when I woke up Sunday morning, all I knew was that I could not spend another day alone with Fern.

I was pleasantly surprised when Cassandra and Marilyn walked over to breakfast with me (followed, of course, by Fern). I was hoping it meant they wouldn't go off together again. But as we ate I couldn't help noticing that the two of them were whispering to each other. They tried to keep their lips from moving, but neither one of them was any good at it.

It happened when I took my tray back. They both left. Fern said they didn't leave a message.

I'd be lying if I said I wasn't hurt. But I have to admit, it wasn't totally unexpected. They were at the end of *their* ropes too. They probably figured they were being nice just having breakfast with Fern and me.

It was time. I didn't even have to think about it anymore. Either Fern had to go, or I would spend the rest of my vacation watching her examine her feet and scrape her teeth. Suddenly the choice didn't seem difficult.

This was it. I would take her back to the cabin and give her the news. Maybe I'd ask her to sit on her bunk. That way, if there was any screaming or crying, I could suggest that she muffle it with a pillow.

"Where're we going, buddy?" she asked, breathing down my neck.

"Back," I answered, matter-of-factly.

I knew she would follow me. I had almost begun to think of myself as Fern's personal magnet.

I'm not sure why, but the trip to the cabin seemed to take longer than usual. Maybe it was because I was walking so slowly. I had to. I wasn't sure what I was going to say when I got there, and I had to give myself time to think.

Unfortunately, even walking slowly, we still got there before I had finished thinking. I stood outside a few seconds and took a deep breath. Fern did the same. It sounded like she needed to blow her nose. I made a face and opened the cabin door.

Once inside, I began pacing nervously, trying to come up with just the right words. What was it I was going to say again? Something about finding her own kind of friends?

Fern stood in the middle of the cabin and followed me with her eyes. She had the kind of eyes that went all around their sockets. It really gave me the creeps.

Just a few more minutes, I thought, starting to get my confidence up. Just a little more thinking time and I'd be ready. I was sure of it.

I climbed up to my bunk.

"Er . . . ah . . . I think I'm going to lie down for a while," I said. "Ah . . . maybe you could go over to arts and crafts and work on your beaver." I knew I could think better if I were alone.

Fern shook her head. "I finished him yesterday. Named him Bucky. His mouth didn't turn out right, but I think I'll just tell people that his dam crashed in on him. Makes him more interesting that way. Like he's a beaver with a story to tell. . . ."

I looked over the edge of the bunk to see if she was kidding. She wasn't. She was busy unzipping her sleeping bag, getting ready to crawl in.

I sighed. It wasn't a perfect solution, but at least if she was down there taking a nap, I wouldn't have to look at her. With any luck at all, and a little quiet, I might be able to figure out everything I wanted to say.

I took another deep breath and tried to think. It wasn't quiet, though. Below me, Fern was rooting around as though she couldn't get comfortable. After a minute or two it almost sounded like she was opening a candy wrapper.

I squeezed my eyes tight shut. I don't know why. Closing your eyes just makes things darker, not quieter.

Suddenly there was no noise at all. I started to breathe a little easier. But then I got the strange feeling that someone was staring at me. I could almost feel their breath on my cheek.

Slowly I opened one eye to look. Fern's face was six inches from my pillow. When she saw me looking at her, she smiled. A large piece of Cracker Jack was lodged between her front teeth.

"Want some?" she asked, offering me the box.

Staring at her in disbelief, I somehow managed a strained "No, thank you."

Fern shrugged and retreated once again to the bottom bunk. I was relieved that she had found something to keep her occupied. If she's eating, it'll keep her quiet for a while, I thought. But *quiet* turned out to be the wrong word. As soon as I heard her chomp down on the first few bites, I recognized the feeling of doom all over again.

I listened in amazement to the assortment of disgusting noises coming from below. If I hadn't known better, I would have sworn that someone had snuck Rollo into the cabin and was feeding him his dinner. Rollo's nice, but he's a pig.

Munch, chomp, munch, crunch . . . The noise was driving me crazy. I covered my head with my pillow and prayed she would eat faster. But the harder I prayed, the more Fern seemed to savor each and every bite, smacking her lips and sucking stubborn little bits of caramel popcorn from the spaces in her teeth.

"Mmmmmm," she murmured, making it even worse. "Mmmm. Mmmmmmm."

I thought I would scream. Where was my mother

when I needed her? This sort of problem was right up her alley. If Mother had been there, she would have snatched the Cracker Jack away so fast it would have made Fern's head spin. Then she would have told her that if she wanted to eat like an animal, she would have to go to her room.

Unfortunately, though, Mother wasn't there. And Fern didn't have her own room. And there was nothing I could do but stuff the edge of my pillow in my mouth and try not to jump down and choke her.

Suddenly the chomping stopped and I listened closely as a new noise took its place. I recognized it right away. It was the sound of a hand digging around in a half-empty Cracker Jack box.

Oh, no, I thought. Please don't let her find it. Just this once . . . *please* don't let her find—

"THE TOY SURPRISE! I FOUND THE TOY SURPRISE! HEY, BUDDY . . . LOOK AT THIS! A LITTLE BITTY PLASTIC WIENER ON A KEY CHAIN!"

I jumped to the floor. There would be time for thinking later. But right at that moment I really felt that if I didn't get out of the cabin I would lose my mind.

I needed to walk. It's a habit I picked up from my father. Whenever he's had a real frustrating day at work, he takes a long walk after dinner. He calls it "clearing his mind." One time, he walked so far that he came home in a police car. I think they picked him up for being a bum. But even so, by the time he walked in the door that night, he was in a better mood. And if any mood needed improving, it was mine.

I probably don't have to mention that Fern was right out the door after me. Luckily she was still admiring her plastic hot dog and wolfing down Cracker Jack, so she was content to follow a few steps behind. She finally asked where we were going, but she didn't seem to mind when I didn't answer.

We ended up at the lake. I had a feeling Cassandra and Marilyn would be there. All week long we had talked about taking a Sunday canoe ride, so I was pretty sure they'd be going ahead with their plans.

I headed straight for the boathouse to check out my suspicion. As I approached the pier I saw them. The two were second in the line of girls waiting for a canoe.

Unfortunately, Fern had seen them first. She darted from behind me and dashed down the pier. She snuck up behind Marilyn, poked her in the back, and shouted, "BOO!"

You couldn't really blame Marilyn for screaming her head off. By the time you're fourteen, most of your friends have finished shouting BOO!, so it was pretty much of a shock. When she finally calmed herself enough to talk, she told Fern that if she wanted to act like a ghost, she should do us all a favor and get run over by a truck.

Fern just smiled. By this time she had stopped taking Marilyn seriously and thought everything that came out of her mouth was some sort of joke.

After the commotion was over, Cass tapped me on

the shoulder and quietly apologized for deserting me again. Marilyn heard her, and nodded. "It's not *you*, Dinah. I hope you know that."

"I know. But if I have to be alone with her again, I think I'll go crazy," I said softly, trying not to move my lips. "I'm not kidding, you guys. It's getting really bad. When we were back at the cabin just now, she was—"

"NEXT!" shouted the counselor. "HOW MANY IN THE NEXT GROUP?"

Cass and Marilyn could tell I was desperate. They just stood there looking at each other. Finally Cass just shrugged and held up four fingers. Marilyn let out a small whimper, but a second later she forced a sick smile to let me know it was all right. I can't remember ever feeling so relieved.

The counselor handed out bright orange life jackets and insisted that we buckle up before getting into the canoe. As soon as we were ready, Marilyn grabbed one of the paddles for herself and handed the other one to me. Cass had already made it clear that she didn't want to handle some slimy old paddle.

"Why don't you get all the way in the back so you can steer," suggested Marilyn. "I'll sit up front and be the guide."

Fern laughed out loud for no reason. We all stared at her. No one said anything, but we all found Fern irritating, and it showed.

Finally Marilyn pushed us away from the dock and started to paddle out to the middle of the lake.

"Hang a right!" she ordered from the front of the canoe.

Rather than admit that I had never steered a canoe before, I stuck my paddle into the water and hoped for the best. When we turned sharply to the left, I shouted a quick "Sorry" and changed sides. Fern was still quietly chuckling to herself. I don't think it had much to do with my paddling, but even so, I felt like telling her to shut up.

Anyway, after a few more mistakes I finally got the hang of it, and we headed out to sea—I mean, to lake. It was really peaceful out there. Fern had finally managed to stop laughing, and with only the sound of the paddles cutting lightly through the water, I actually began to enjoy myself for the first time all day.

We glided along for several minutes before we ran into our first problem. That's when Fern's feet began to sweat.

"My toes are sticking together," she whined, reaching down to pull off her shoes.

"P.U.! The sun really makes your feet stink, doesn't it?" she went on, yanking off one sock and then the other.

Before anyone knew what to expect, she had swung her stinky feet over the side of the canoe and was trying to dangle them in the water. When they didn't reach, she pulled them back in again and pushed her smelly sneakers away from her, toward Cassandra.

"P.U.! PEWIE!" Fern hollered.

I think it was on the "PEWIE" that Cassandra finally blew up. Normally, she wasn't a very loud person, but when she finally let go, you could hear her blood-curdling howl all over the lake. I'm not sure if she did it to be funny, or just to let off steam. But whatever it was, it was so unusual that Marilyn and I couldn't help but laugh. Fern began to laugh too. I almost felt sorry for her. She was still under the impression that we were all having a good time.

After Cassandra finished screaming, I tried to force the calm, peaceful feeling back again, but I knew it wouldn't work. Getting into the canoe with Fern had been a mistake. She was only one person, but it was as if she had us surrounded. We couldn't pretend she wasn't there. We couldn't even pretend she was funny. She was getting on our nerves like never before, and it wasn't fair to any of us. Not to Marilyn, or Cass, or me . . . and not to Fern, either. Especially not to Fern. I could see that now, more clearly than ever before. She had to be told the truth, and it had to be done quickly. As soon as we got back to the dock, there would be no more excuses. No more backing out.

Almost without thinking, I slipped my paddle into the water and held it steady to turn the canoe around. Puzzled, Marilyn looked back. When she saw me pointing to the dock, relief spread across her face. She mouthed the words *Thank you* and smiled in appreciation.

Once we were pointed toward the boathouse, we started paddling faster and faster. Suddenly I just couldn't get there quickly enough. Our canoe zipped through the water as the two of us pressed on, full steam ahead.

"Hey!" said Fern excitedly. "Where's the fire?"

Marilyn and I ignored the question. By this time, we were more than halfway there.

"Hey!" she said again. "Where're we going?"

Finally Marilyn looked over her shoulder. "Back!" she snapped, still paddling furiously.

"Back? But I haven't even had a turn to paddle yet. Can't I paddle too?"

Fern repeated this question at least four times and then got more insistent. "Hold it. Stop! We're almost there. Come on, you guys. Let me paddle a second!"

All of a sudden, Marilyn turned sharply in her seat. "Oh, all right!" she growled. "If Fern just *has* to paddle, she can paddle. Stop the stupid boat and change places with her, Dinah. It'll be easier for her to steer us into the dock from the back seat."

Fern bolted up excitedly. Her sudden movement rocked the canoe, and she nearly lost her balance. She had to grab the sides to keep from falling overboard.

It was one of those things I wish I had never seen. But I had. And it gave me an idea so terrible, I got a sick feeling in the pit of my stomach. Slowly I raised my head and looked around me. First at Cass, then at Marilyn. They stared at me intently. In their eyes I could see the same horrible thought.

Meanwhile, Fern was wobbling toward me. She wasn't that far away, but the way she walked made it obvious that she didn't exactly have sea legs. Instead of proceeding confidently, she teetered nervously as she inched her way closer. She was holding her smelly sneakers in one hand, which couldn't have helped her balance any.

I stood up carefully and waited. Marilyn coughed to get my attention. When I looked back at her, she made a small pushing gesture. Cass saw her and nodded her head in approval. Their silent message was clear: Push her! Push her, Dinah! Just this once, and it'll all be over. . . .

I began to sweat. I could feel the wetness in my hands. Fern was almost next to me. She was reaching out to take the paddle.

"NOW!"

Marilyn's command shattered the awful silence. I didn't have time to think. I just lunged for Fern's shoulder and gave her a hard shove.

She fell backward into the water. She didn't say a word. She didn't even scream. She just stared at me for a split second and then she was gone.

But in that instant, just as she was about to hit the water, her eyes focused right on mine. And in those eyes I saw more hurt than I had ever thought possible.

« 9 »

We didn't get in trouble. As soon as we pulled alongside the dock, Marilyn told the counselor that Fern had accidentally fallen overboard, and we couldn't get her back in the canoe.

I'm not sure she believed us. But instead of arguing, she grabbed a life preserver and tossed it to Fern, who was still bobbing up and down silently in the water.

We didn't stick around to watch Fern being reeled in. Quietly Marilyn suggested that we "lay low" for a while. Without another word, Cassandra and I followed her to a small toolshed on the opposite side of the camp. She said it would make a good hideout in case Fern decided to squeal.

"Don't look so glum, Dinah," Marilyn said reassuringly. "It's just like we talked about before. It'll probably hurt her for a little while at first, but in the long run it's the best thing you could have done . . . for her as well as for us."

"You didn't see the look on her face," I replied. "Oh, Marilyn, it was awful."

94

Cassandra put her arm around me. "She was just surprised, that's all."

For some reason her comment annoyed me. "It was *hurt*, Cass. I'm thirteen years old. I think I know the difference between hurt and surprise."

After snapping at Cassandra like that, I couldn't make polite conversation. We just sat in the shed for the next hour or so, listening to each other breathe. Whenever someone walked by outside, Marilyn would put her finger to her lips and say, "Shh!" But how can you get any quieter than breathing? If we had been talking, I probably would have snapped at her.

We all seemed to get tired of sitting there at the same time. Marilyn went out first and gave us an "all clear" signal. To tell you the truth, she was beginning to get on my nerves. I had just done the meanest thing of my life, and she was acting like we were in a Davy Crockett adventure movie.

Just to make sure Fern hadn't squealed, Marilyn casually wandered by the boathouse and waved to the counselor still on duty. When she waved back, we knew we were safe.

Cassandra breathed a huge sigh of relief and gave me a hug. My arms weren't in the mood for hugging back and hung limply at my sides.

This time Cass looked concerned. "Look. I know what we did wasn't great, but you've really got to stop taking it so hard. It wasn't all your fault, you know. If Fern hadn't insisted on being so weird, none of this would have ever happened. Don't you see? Sometimes you just have to take a stand against the Fern Wadleys of the world. If you don't, you'll end up with a whole slew of nerds and leeches hanging on to you wherever you go. How does that sound?"

I rolled my eyes disgustedly. "Like a scene from *Swamp Thing*."

"Stop acting like that, Dinah. I'm trying to make a point here," she retorted. "Haven't you ever seen that commercial? You know, the one that says you only go around once in life? Well, all I'm saying is, what's so horrible about wanting to go around with people that you like? Why is that so wrong?"

This time I didn't roll my eyes. I knew I had no right to be mad at Cass. I was the one who had done the pushing, not her. *I* was the one I was really angry at.

I looked at her a minute and sighed. "I *know* you're trying to make me feel better, but could we please just change the subject? Who knows, maybe someday I'll take a lot of pride in knowing I pushed an unsuspecting, innocent person into Lake Miniwawa. But right now I think I'd like to try and forget about it."

We all tried to forget about it. Or at least we pretended to forget. When we finally went back to the cabin that afternoon, we pretended not to see the huge lump shivering inside Fern's sleeping bag with a pillow over its head. Her wet clothes hung from the railing at the end of her bunk, but we pretended not to see the large puddle of water they were making on the cabin floor. We stepped over it, of course, but we pretended not to see it. Then, later on that night as we were trying to get to sleep, we pretended we couldn't hear the *drip* . . . *drip* . . . *drip* of water running out of Fern's shorts onto the cement floor. That is, most of us pretended.

"Where the heck's that darned dripping coming from?" hollered Crystal, bolting up in her bed. "Somebody fix it. It's driving me crazy!"

Without saying a word, Fern got out of bed and laid her drippy shorts next to her waterlogged shoes. When she crawled back into her bunk, she sneezed.

Crystal said, "Gesundheit."

Cass and Marilyn and I pretended not to hear.

When we woke up the next morning Fern was already gone.

"ANYONE SEEN THAT ONE WITH THE BANGS IN HER FACE?" bellowed Maggie. She still didn't know Fern's name.

"Yeah. She was headed for chow hall about ten minutes ago," offered Crystal on her way out the door. "Had on squishy sneakers. What'd she do . . . swim in 'em?"

The sick feeling came over me again. I hadn't really expected that just one night's sleep would make me forget about what I had done; but if anything, I seemed to feel worse.

It was pretty obvious that Cass and Marilyn were better pretenders than I was. Even though we saw Fern, eating her breakfast alone, they were extra careful not to mention her name. Instead they talked about how gross the food was. Naturally, if it had been as bad as they said, they wouldn't have been at the table in the first place. But even so, if you ever want to have a long conversation, disgusting camp food is one of the best topics you can choose. You can talk for hours and not cover it all.

After breakfast we all went outside and talked about which activities we would sign up for that day.

"What would you like to do today, Dinah?" asked Marilyn, pretending to be cheerful.

I shrugged. "Maybe I could go down to the pier and push some of the little kids off the dock."

Marilyn just shook her head and signed us up for horseback riding and archery lessons.

I guess I don't need to mention that my heart wasn't really in it. Also, the horses didn't help any. They were older than my parents. It was really stupid. They all had names like Lightning and Wildfire, but with a saddle and a kid on top of them, it was all they could do to walk. Marilyn said most of them hadn't galloped since about 1960. After they walked a mile or so, they started to drool so much, we had to get off and let them rest. The counselor said they were "frothing," but I know drool when I see it. All in all, I've had more exciting rides on a merry-go-round.

After the riding, I figured archery lessons sounded pretty good. But as it turned out, the "lesson" part was a lie. There was no instructor. Instead there was just this cooking lady from the dining hall, sitting in a lawn chair reading a book.

"Archery instructor's sick," she muttered when she saw us coming. "You can practice on your own if you promise not to shoot yourselves."

Marilyn hurried over and picked up a bow that was lying on the ground. "Don't worry, there's nothing to it," she announced.

People who are good at something are always saying "Nothing to it." The first time I tried to do a back-bend, Deena said there was nothing to it, and then stood there and watched me fall over on my head.

After twenty minutes my longest-traveling arrow was only three feet in front of me. The rest of them were in a pile at my feet. That's when I threw down my bow and announced that I was going back to the cabin. Cassandra and Marilyn stopped what they were doing long enough to wave. They really seemed to be having a good time. I honestly don't think they were pretending anymore.

On the way back all I could concentrate on was the cabin in the distance. "Oh, *please*. Just let it be empty," I said out loud.

When I finally got there and found I was alone, I closed my eyes and said, "Thank you." I'm not sure who I was thanking. I mean, I doubt that God had interrupted his busy schedule to clear the cabin for me. But I closed my eyes and said it anyway.

I napped most of the afternoon and didn't see Fern again until dinner. She didn't come back to the cabin to wash up or anything. Not that she ever spent that much time washing up, but at least she usually stood around the sinks watching the rest of us.

At dinner I was halfway through my cold spaghetti when I saw her come in the door and get in the food line. She didn't look at us when she passed by with her tray. She didn't stop for a second and try to pinch anyone or say BOO! She just kept her head down and headed for a table in the corner to eat by herself.

I couldn't help wondering where she had been all day. She hadn't gone swimming. That was for sure. She didn't know how, and besides, she had no buddy . . . nobody. She had already finished her beaver in arts and crafts, and she couldn't play shuffleboard by herself. She could have gone riding, of course, but who'd want to? And she certainly couldn't archer, or whatever they call shooting arrows. Even *I* couldn't archer.

I turned my attention to Marilyn and Cass, who had pretended not to see Fern when she walked by. I thought about asking how they could keep acting like that, but then I didn't bother. After all, once you got the hang of it, there was probably "nothing to it."

Cassandra glanced in my direction. "Did you say something?"

"Er . . . yeah. Ah, how 'bout if we play some shuffleboard after dinner?"

Actually I hated shuffleboard, but the thought of going back to the cabin and facing Fern made me very uncomfortable. She'd probably be sitting there, looking pitiful, with spaghetti all over her face.

I'm not sure how many games of shuffleboard we played that night. But when it finally got too dark to see, we were all pretty sick of it. Especially Marilyn. She was the loser.

"The ninny who invented this stupid game was probably the same guy who invented hopscotch. I hate that, too," she muttered.

Fern was already in bed when we returned. She was facing the screens, so I didn't have to see the spaghetti on her face. That made it easier. But not much.

«10»

The next morning after breakfast Cass and Marilyn
went to sign up for swimming. They wanted me to
come along, but I told them I had to write a letter.

It wasn't the truth. I really wanted to go for a walk.
Alone. I hadn't slept that well the night before and I
wasn't in the mood for clowning around in the water
with the two of them. I can't explain it, but no matter
how much you like your friends, sometimes you're still
your own best company.

I don't know how far I walked that morning. Lots of
miles, though, I'm pretty sure of that. Eventually all of
the hiking trails at Miniwawa run into each other at the
softball field, so every time I'd come to the field, I'd
circle around again. It was very peaceful walking alone
like that, and by the time I had circled around for my
last trip, I decided I would walk with my dad once in a
while when I got home.

When I was finally ready to head back to civilization,
I'm sure at least two hours had passed. But before I

started for the cabin, I stopped under one of the huge pine trees lining the trail to rest for a minute.

That's when I heard the sneeze. It came from behind a rock, several yards to my right. A second later it was followed by a snort, a gross snort I would have recognized anywhere. It was Fern's gross snort, of course. And as I listened, the forest was filled with the sound of loud nose-blowing. I made a face and prayed silently that she was using a tissue.

What was she doing there, anyway? Hiding? Spying on me? Or maybe she didn't even know I was around. Maybe she had found a new friend, and they were hiking together. My curiosity was getting the best of me, and I *had* to know.

Slyly, I ducked behind the huge pine and waited for her to make a move. But nothing happened. Not even another sneeze. She was still there, though. I could see the top of her head poking up from behind the rock. And I decided that if I wanted to find out what she was doing there, I would have to make the first move myself.

I've always been good at spying on people. I think it's one of those talents you either have or you don't. It's not something I practice. I just automatically seem to know when to duck down, when to peek, stuff like that. It doesn't sound hard, but I think you have to be spied on by someone who's a klutz before you appreciate it. Wanda tried to spy on me once, and the first time I turned around, she was half in and half out of Mrs. Trebolina's trash can.

103

I stayed hidden for several minutes before I finally circled around my tree and tiptoed through the leafy brush. I'm excellent on leafy brush. The secret is to watch your feet and not breathe.

I ended up behind another tree at a slightly different angle. Fern was still partly hidden behind her rock, but now I could see some of her body. Her arms and legs, mostly. She was sitting cross-legged, playing with a couple of leaves. After a while she picked up a stick and drew a picture in the dirt. But mostly she just sat.

As I stood there watching, the same sick feeling that had hit me the day before hit me again. She wasn't spying at all, or hiding, or anything else I had imagined. She was just sitting there in the woods, all by herself, waiting for the day to pass. No new friends, no one her own style to feel "comfortable" with. It was just Fern and a stick, sitting behind a rock. And I can't remember ever feeling as low as I did that day, peering at her from my hiding place.

How I wished I hadn't found her there! Why did I have to see? But more than that, why did I have to meet her in the first place?

If only I had come to camp a week earlier or a week later. If only I hadn't been the first one at the stupid bus stop that day, none of this would have happened.

If only Hubby hadn't insisted that Fern go to camp, or Ilsa had taught her not to pick her feet in public. If only she hadn't cleared out her nostrils, or chewed with her mouth open, or scraped her teeth with her fingernail. If only she hadn't swung me around and around in the cabin, or pinched people under the table, or pounded Cass to the floor. If only she hadn't gone crazy over a little fake wiener key chain, or followed me to the canoe, or yelled BOO! and scared Marilyn half to death. If only she hadn't taken her shoes off in the boat, or shouted PEWIE! at the top of her lungs, or insisted on paddling. *Why* had she insisted on paddling? Oh, God! *Why did she have to paddle?*

If only I hadn't pushed . . .

I *had* to get out of there. I just couldn't watch her for one more second. What was I supposed to do, anyway? Sit down beside her and say, "I'm sorry I pushed you, let's be pals?" Well, maybe I should have, but I just couldn't.

This time I didn't even try to tiptoe back through the leafy brush. I just ran out of there as fast as I could, not stopping to wonder who could see me or who couldn't and not even caring.

It wasn't fair. Fern was gone now. She was officially "dumped," but somehow she was *still* ruining things for me. Even safely hidden behind a rock, she was making me miserable. Why did it have to be this way?

Suddenly I stopped. I hadn't planned to stop. I mean, I hadn't been slowing down or anything. But something inside my head said, "Wait!" So I stopped and waited.

"Maybe it *doesn't* have to be this way," it continued. "You aren't really going to let her do this to you again, are you? You aren't actually going to let her ruin *another* day! And how about tomorrow, and the next day?

105

Are you going to let her spoil those, too? Hasn't she ruined enough, Dinah? Hasn't she nearly driven you crazy with her gross manners and almost single-handedly spoiled your friendship with Cass and Marilyn? Didn't she cause you to do the meanest thing you've ever done in your life? Well, didn't she? And isn't that enough? Does she get to wreck the rest of your vacation too?"

It was really strange. Normally, when I feel sorry for someone, my insides turn to mush. But this time I was getting angry, and my thoughts seemed to be coming from a tougher side of my brain. I didn't feel like Dinah Feeney, The Kind One. Instead, I felt like Dinah Feeney looking out for Dinah Feeney.

Or maybe *tough* was the wrong word. Maybe for once in my life, I was being fair to myself for a change—or kind. That was okay, wasn't it? You can be kind to yourself, too, can't you?

I started to walk slowly. Then faster and faster, until before long I was running. But now I was running down to the lake to be with my friends, the friends Fern had almost made me lose.

Cass and Marilyn had just gotten out of the water when I spotted them. They were standing on the edge of the dock, getting ready to dry off.

I slowed down for a minute and looked all around. The lifeguard on duty had her back to us, talking to another counselor. I began to laugh quietly to myself, knowing what I was about to do. Then, using my quick but silent spy feet, I snuck up behind Cass and Marilyn and pushed them both back into the water, towels and all.

Cass came up sputtering. I guess she had gotten water up her nose. It was red and drippy, and she kept trying to blow the water back out. She didn't look very attractive, but she looked human, and I liked her that way.

When Marilyn finally surfaced, she wiped the hair out of her eyes and tapped her fingers on the top of the water.

"Thanks, I needed that," she muttered sarcastically.

I stopped laughing long enough to lean down and help them back up to the pier. I should have known better, of course. As soon as Marilyn had my hand, she gave it a hard tug and pulled me headfirst into the water, fully dressed.

Now it was their turn to laugh. When I came up for air, Cassandra pushed me back under again.

It was dark down there. And for just a split second, a picture of Fern sitting all alone behind her rock tried to sneak into my head and ruin my fun. But the tough side of my brain was ready and squeezed it back out.

When I came up the second time, I started laughing all over again.

With the tough side of my brain coming to my rescue all day, having fun with Cass and Marilyn turned out to be so easy, I could hardly believe it. I guess I should have known right away there would be a catch. Anytime something's *that* easy, there's always a catch. Take selling Christmas cards door-to-door, for instance. When you send off for them, the company makes it sound like you're going to be a millionaire in a week. Then they send you Christmas cards so ugly you can hardly even pawn them off on your relatives.

I didn't find out about the catch until later that night. It was dark and quiet in the cabin, and I had just rolled over to go to sleep. That's when it hit me. *The tough side of my brain goes to sleep before the rest of me.*

I'm not kidding. I don't know where it went or what it was doing. All I know is that as I was lying there in the dark, with all that time to think, I could feel that sick guilty feeling starting all over again. Only *this* time, I couldn't find the toughness. And when you can't find the toughness, pictures of all the mean things you've done can dance in and out of your mind, with nothing there to stop them. It was as if all the anger I had had for Fern earlier had gone off duty. And I knew that if I couldn't stay mad at her, this time I was doomed for sure.

What is it about anger, anyway? Why can't something that sounds so tough be a little more durable? I should have remembered that anger never makes it through the night. Once, I decided that I wouldn't speak to my mother for the rest of my life, and the next morning I got right out of bed and asked her for the Rice Krispies.

Without my tough side, it wasn't easy, but I tried to get my thoughts under control.

Stop thinking about it! I ordered. There's nothing to feel guilty about. You're acting as if sitting behind a rock is the worst thing in the world. I bet there are thousands of people all over the country who would love to spend a quiet, peaceful day relaxing behind a cool rock in the middle of the forest. Millions, probably.

After all, Fern wasn't chained to a dungeon wall or buried up to her neck in an anthill. She could still get up and make new friends if she wanted to. What was I making the big deal about? I bet the tough side of my brain wouldn't bother feeling guilty for a second. If the tough side of my brain were here it would just say, "You're making a mountain out of a molehill. Now, shut up and get some sleep." Sure it would . . . of course . . . not another thought . . .

I shut my eyes. But sleep didn't come for a long, long time.

The next morning was mail call. I heard Maggie's wake-up whistle, but I was still pretty groggy when my first letter hit me in the cheek.

"Ow!" I yelled.

It didn't hurt, but I yelled anyway. In my opinion, Maggie could have found a nicer way of delivering letters than sailing them through the air like Frisbees.

"BARNHILL, BARNHILL, FEENEY, BALL, WADLEY, BARNHILL, FEENEY, POWERS, FEENEY, AND BALL!" she called as she launched them one by one.

109

Marilyn caught hers in midair and stared at it in disbelief. "That's it?" she questioned. "Just one? Just one lousy little letter from home for the entire week?"

"Face it, Marilyn," teased Cass, "they don't like you."

"I know. But that doesn't mean I shouldn't get mail. Even mass murderers get mail."

Then, without saying another word, she stormed angrily across the cabin and shoved the screen door open.

"THANKS A LOT, MOM AND DAD!" she screeched at the top of her lungs. "I GET OUT OF YOUR LIVES FOR A COUPLE OF WEEKS, AND *THIS* IS THE THANKS I GET? ONE LOUSY LITTLE LETTER?"

She headed back to her bunk, still muttering. "All I've got to say is, there better be money in it."

I looked at the letters in front of me. After listening to poor Marilyn, I felt almost embarrassed that there were three of them. They didn't turn out to be especially thrilling, though. The first one was from Wanda. She said that summer was even more boring by herself than it was with me. I think it was supposed to be a compliment, but it's hard to tell for sure. Then she said we'd hang out again as soon as I got home. We stopped calling it "playing" when we got to junior high.

The other two were from my mother. Since she had also sent me two letters the previous week, there wasn't much news. She mentioned that Rollo didn't seem to be scratching his sore place as much lately and that Aunt Maude had bought a new cane with a genuine gold handle. I realize that it's not easy to come up with a lot of neat stuff for letters, but I still think she could have done better than the latest cane news. As usual, she signed the letters "Love, Mother and Dad."

"Why does she do that?" I wondered out loud. "Why does she always sign her letters 'Mother and Dad'? My father didn't write one word of this letter. He probably doesn't even know she sent it."

Cassandra stopped reading long enough to answer my question. "I asked my mother the same thing once when she was signing Christmas cards. She said she puts Pop's name on them so people won't know she's married to an inconsiderate clod."

Suddenly, on the other side of the room, Marilyn let out a loud groan. "They call *this* a letter?" Then she held it up in front of her and started reading:

"Dear Marilyn,
There's not too much to write about this week, but I wanted you to have a letter to open so I'm sending this anyway. Hope you're having a good time, and please don't come home with dirt ground into your underwear like you did last year.

Love,
Mom and Daddy"

I couldn't tell if Marilyn was really upset or if she was just pretending. But either way, her letter sounded so funny, I couldn't help laughing.

Finally I crawled out of my sleeping bag and got

ready to jump down. Since I didn't know where Fern was, I was careful not to put my feet on her bunk. But after I had landed on the floor, I was surprised to see that she wasn't in her bunk at all.

"Where's F—" I said before catching myself, but no one was paying much attention anyway. I strolled quietly over to the cabin door and looked out.

I saw her in the distance hurrying down the path toward her rock. Almost running, really. She had an envelope in her hand.

«11»

Fern carried the letter with her for days. The first few times I saw her with it, I figured she had forgotten to put it away. But when she was still reading it the second night as she sat all alone at dinner, I got the feeling that she was acting weird. I wasn't the only one who thought so.

"Have either of you guys noticed you-know-who, in the corner over there?" asked Cass as we sat down to supper. "That's about the millionth time I've seen her read that letter in the past couple of days. Not that I watch her that much, but at practically every meal, she's had that piece of paper plastered to her eyeballs."

Marilyn squinted. "Oh, no. Her lips are moving. Please, someone, tell me that she isn't *talking* to it."

"She isn't talking to it, Marilyn. She's reading it," I replied, trying to sound sure of myself. If Fern was so lonely that she had started talking to a letter, I, for one, certainly didn't want to know about it.

"What could anyone write that would be that inter-

113

esting?" asked Cass again. "Even the letters *I* got were only good for three or four readings."

"You're lucky," I confessed. "My mother's letters were barely good for one."

"Oh, mine weren't from my mother. They were from my friends. One was from Muffy. One was from Bunny. And the third one was from Buffy."

Marilyn stared across the table in complete disbelief. "Could you run those names by me one more time?"

Cassandra shrugged. "Muffy, Bunny, and Buffy."

Marilyn covered her mouth with her hand. "Excuse me. I think I'm going to barfy."

"What's wrong with *you*?" Cass asked, sounding offended.

"Those names!" Laughing, Marilyn held up her hand. "Don't tell me. They all live down the road from Farmer McGregor's garden with their brother, Peter Rabbit. Am I right?"

By this time it was plain to see that Cass was angry. "For your information, Miss Comedian, we happened to make up those names ourselves because they sounded better than their *real* names. Even their *mothers* are using them now. At least, Buffy's and Bunny's mothers are. Muffy's is still holding out."

"Tuffy," giggled Marilyn.

"What's the name you gave yourself?" I asked quickly, hoping to get Cassandra's mind off Marilyn. But the question only seemed to annoy her even more.

"Mine didn't *need* changing," she snapped.

"How about Fluffy? Fluffy would be nice," offered Marilyn, who was almost hysterical.

That did it. I had just taken a sip of milk and almost spit it out on the table. Cass bolted right up from the table and stalked off with her tray. I could tell by the look in her eye that she was really fuming. When she passed the table on her way out the door, she stopped for a second and glared first at me, then at Marilyn. Quickly, I dabbed a few milk dribbles from my chin.

"Did anyone ever tell you that you guys can be real jerks sometimes?" she growled.

But Marilyn was too far gone to settle down. "No need to get *huffy*," she roared. Only this time, she was laughing so hard she fell off the bench.

Cassandra stormed out of the dining hall without saying another word. I'm not sure how long Marilyn stayed on the floor laughing like that. When someone's making a spectacle of themselves, it always seems like it's going on longer than it really is. Even so, the whole episode was pretty hysterical.

Finally, Marilyn got up and dusted herself off. "Sorry. I just couldn't seem to help myself there for a minute."

"I noticed," I replied, still chuckling.

"Yeah. Well, maybe I better go find her and smooth things over for us. After all, it was mostly my fault, and there's no sense blowing the friendship the last couple of days."

115

"I'll be there when I'm finished," I assured her.

After watching Marilyn leave, my eyes automatically drifted back over to Fern again. She was just putting her letter back in its envelope. It was part of her routine. First she would take it out and read it. Then she would smile for a few seconds and put it back in the envelope. A few minutes later she'd start the whole thing all over again.

I knew I shouldn't just sit there and stare at her all night, but for some reason it made me feel better to watch. Especially when she got to the part where she smiled. What had been written that made her so happy? Was it from her mother? Had she promised that they'd do something special when she got home? Had she bought her a surprise?

Well, whatever it was, I was glad Fern had received the letter. I know I was being selfish, but each time I saw her smile, it seemed to take a little bit more of my guilt away. After all, I couldn't have ruined her life *that* badly. Not if she could sit there and grin at a letter that way.

I sat there watching her as long as I could, but after a while the dining hall began to clear out, and I knew I'd have to leave. I mean, it's easy spying on someone across a room full of people, but when you're left sitting at a table all by yourself, even the best spy in the world looks a little conspicuous.

I put my tray away and headed for the door. But before I left, I gave Fern one last glance out of the corner of my eye. She was in her smiling stage. And although I knew I should probably just keep walking, it was hard to take my eyes away.

Smile back! I don't know where the order came from but it took me by surprise. Smile back! That'll make her feel better about things. It'll be good for both of you. Do it, quick! Before you lose your nerve!

Almost without my telling them to, my feet carried me over to her table. I was only a few feet away when I felt the smile begin to spread across my face. It was probably one of the biggest smiles my mouth has ever managed. Sort of like a jack-o'-lantern, only not as orange.

I cleared my throat loudly. Fern looked up. And although it seemed impossible, I stretched my grin even farther.

Fern didn't smile back. She didn't even come close. Instead, she jumped up from the bench and pointed her finger at me.

"STAY AWAY FROM ME! DO YOU HEAR?" she screamed. "JUST STAY AWAY!" A second later she was out the door.

It all happened so fast, I was left standing there with most of the giant smile still on my face. I guess I was in shock or something. I could hear a lot of whispering going on behind me, but my legs didn't seem to want to turn around and face it.

"What's going on here?" demanded a loud voice from out of nowhere. A second later I was looking into the angry face of the dining-hall manager. "What'd you *do* to that poor girl?"

117

"Nothing! I ... er .. . I was just smiling. Ah ... see? I think most of it's still up there."

The manager wasn't amused. "GET OUT OF HERE, YOU!"

She called me "you." I hate to be called "you." It's as though I'm not even good enough to be called a name.

"Yeah, well, I guess I'll just be running along now. 'Bye," I said, trying to act like the whole thing was a joke. But on the inside, I was dying. And when I finally left the building, I was shaking all over and I felt like throwing up.

I didn't, though. Instead I started walking so fast, the breeze in my face must have snapped me out of it. I felt the anger coming back. Only this time, not just part of me was angry. *All* of me was angry.

Why did she have to humiliate me like that? All I wanted to do was smile!

Wasn't smiling supposed to make things better? Anyone knows that! Even *babies* know that! Some baby smiled at my dad in a restaurant once, and he gave her his crackers! What was it he had said that day? Give a smile away and it'll always come back? Something like that, anyway. . . .

Wrong again, Dad. Thanks a lot. Great little piece of advice, but let's get it right the next time, huh? How about, Give a smile away and Fern will ruin your day? How's that for a catchy little saying?

I'm not sure how long I wandered around getting mad at people. But I went through almost everyone I know. That happens sometimes when you're angry. Even people you haven't seen in years have to take some of the blame.

When I finally went back to the cabin, I had settled down a little, but I still wasn't ready to see Fern again. I was very relieved when I peeked through the cabin screen and discovered Fern wasn't there.

"Dinah!" yelled Cassandra as soon as I opened the door. Then, before I knew what hit me, she ran over and flung her arms around me.

Puzzled, I looked at Marilyn.

She shrugged. "We made up," she mouthed.

"Of course we made up!" exclaimed Cassandra. "And now we've just been sitting around talking about how much we're going to miss each other. Haven't we, Marlo?"

Marilyn's face turned red. "I didn't say to *call* me that," she sputtered. "I only said I *liked* it. Besides, it was supposed to be confidential."

Even Marilyn dreams of changing her name! I couldn't help but laugh. I was really going to miss both of them. Even after everything that had happened, knowing them and being their friend had been fun.

"Anyway," continued Marilyn, "there's no sense getting all sentimental *now*. We've still got the banquet dinner tomorrow night, don't forget."

"I can't help feeling sad," replied Cassandra, sitting down next to Marilyn and hugging her. "I'm just really going to miss you guys, that's all."

After giving Marilyn another squeeze, she motioned

119

for me to join them. I didn't want to, though. The truth is that even though I think I'm pretty sensitive about most things, I don't go in for a lot of mushy good-byes. I hardly ever get weepy or cry like most people do. I guess when you've got emotional parents, you learn to control your feelings. When my aunt and uncle moved to Boston, I was the only cousin at the farewell party who didn't have to blow her nose. I think they must have noticed, too. That was the first Christmas that they didn't put money in my card.

Marilyn was right about the farewell banquet Friday night. We weren't even in the dining hall before Cassandra started checking to make sure she had her tissues with her. Marilyn and I had to tell her "Chin up" at least a thousand times before the night was over.

Thinking back, I still don't know where they got the nerve to call it a banquet. It was the same kind of food we had every other night, only this time they had put paper tablecloths over all the picnic tables. Also, we got to drink out of green plastic glasses instead of milk cartons. Whoopee.

It might have fooled the younger kids, but it didn't fool us for a minute. As Marilyn put it, "You can put slop on any kind of tablecloth you want, but it's still slop."

All the counselors were sitting at the head table. Everyone else was supposed to be grouped by cabins. Naturally Crystal paid no attention to the rules and sat with her friends from cabin 13.

120

Fern was sitting at a table in the corner. I was still mad at her, but it didn't keep me from looking around to see where she was. I guess curiosity is the strongest feeling of them all.

Besides, as long as I was mad, I was pretty sure that seeing her sitting alone wouldn't bother me much. That's what happens when someone humiliates you. You lose a lot of your compassion. And anyway, this time Fern wasn't exactly alone. She was sitting with six little Daffy Ducklings. There weren't talking to her, but a couple of them were staring like they were trying to figure out where she had come from.

"What do you keep stretching your neck to look at, Dinah?" asked Cassandra, taking me by surprise.

"Er . . . ah . . . nothing," I answered, trying to think fast. "I read somewhere that if you stretch your neck muscles a lot when you're young, you won't get a double chin when you're old."

When the meal finally came, I turned my attention back to the table. I guess you'd call it a meal. The official name for it was Camper's Cuisine.

"Cuisine, my eyeball!" grumbled Marilyn. "Don't let the fancy French name fool you. I'd recognize this gunk anywhere. It's the same gunk they had last year, only then they called it Diner's Delight. All it is, is a slab of mystery meat with some rotten vegetables thrown in. It's the same garbage hobos eat, only *they* call it hobo's stew. If you're a shepherd, I think they call it shepherd's pie. Any way you look at it, it's slop." Just hearing her talk about it took my appetite away.

After dessert (a hard brown object called Camper's Cupcake), the head counselor began tapping on her glass to get our attention. I don't know why she didn't just scream "SHUT UP!" and get it over with.

Suddenly Jill, the piano player, struck up a tune, and all the counselors began swaying back and forth as they sang the official camp farewell song. Maggie went from table to table passing out word sheets:

Now is the hour when we must say good-bye,
Soon we'll be heading far away from here. . . .
Please don't be sad, please don't cry,
Dear Miniwawa, we'll be back next year.

"Over my dead body," added Marilyn after the first chorus.

We had to sing the stupid thing about a thousand times. We were supposed to all join hands and sway along with the counselors. Then, when it was finally over, we were supposed to go around to all the different tables hugging everybody good-bye. I'm talking about people we hadn't even said hello to yet.

Cass was gone in a flash. A lot of people seemed interested in hugging her. Marilyn and I sat down on the bench. She was more like me when it came to the sentimental stuff.

"I like to save my tears for things that really matter," she explained. "You know, like throwing a fit when I want a new sweater . . . stuff like that."

Even so, while we sat there, a lot of girls I hardly

122

knew came up and said good-bye to us. Most of them even knew my name. All of them knew Marilyn's, but then again, *my* grandfather didn't own the camp. One kid even asked if Marilyn could sneak her in free next year. When Marilyn glared at her, the girl finally said "Ha, ha," but I could tell she hadn't really been kidding.

While Marilyn was shaking a few more hands, my curiosity got the best of me again, and I hopped up on the bench to look for Fern. I didn't think there was much danger of being noticed in the midst of all the hugging and confusion. And besides, I was practically positive Fern would have already left.

I was wrong, though. When I stood on my tiptoes and stretched my neck to see over the crowd, I spotted her with no trouble at all. And like so many times before, I immediately wished I hadn't.

She was standing alone at the end of her table, leaning over in case one of the little Daffy Ducklings wanted to hug her.

None of them did.

«12»

The buses came at ten o'clock. There were more of them than I remembered, but with so many girls going in so many different directions, I guess it made sense. Cassandra and Marilyn and I weren't going to get to ride home together. They were going north. I was going south.

As the bus driver was loading the luggage for the trip home, the three of us said our last good-byes. We exchanged phone numbers and addresses. Then Cass threw her arms around me and patted my back for about ten minutes. If I had been a baby, I probably would have burped. I thought about doing it anyway, but I'm not sure she would have seen the humor in it.

When she was finally finished, there were tears running down her cheeks. In a way, it made me feel bad. I pretended to sniffle so it wouldn't seem so one-sided.

As Cass was searching through her purse for a tissue, I said good-bye to Marilyn. I would miss her. But there was no sense kidding myself. The three of us would probably never see each other again. And although I

124

had loved being part of their relationship, it hadn't always been that easy. I didn't regret their friendship, but I had paid a big price for it. And deep inside, I think I was ready to leave.

"I'll call you sometime," I said, giving her a quick squeeze. I wasn't sure I really would, but it's the kind of promise you make when you're leaving, whether you plan to keep it or not.

Marilyn smiled and rumpled the top of my hair. "Yeah. Sure, kiddo. See you around."

Normally I don't like being called "kiddo," but when Marilyn said it, it made me feel good. I rumpled her hair in return.

While all of this was going on, Maggie Blocker was rushing around behind us blowing her whistle like crazy. Maybe she had a quota to fill and hadn't gotten all her *tweets* in yet. When I walked over to tell her good-bye, she didn't even take it out of her mouth. She just shook my hand, gave me a farewell toot, and that was that.

I was first on the bus. This time, though, I chose a seat near the middle. A lot of the girls filing in behind me said hi as they passed by; some I didn't even know. Finally, a little girl from the Daffy Ducklings sat down in the seat next to me.

"Hi," I said at my very friendliest.

But instead of answering, she just stared into my face. Then suddenly she snapped her fingers.

"You're that Dinah from the talent show, aren't you?" she asked excitedly.

125

When I nodded, she giggled. "You were really good!"

I leaned back casually in my seat and smiled smugly. "Good, huh?"

"Yeah. A lot of the girls in my cabin thought you guys acted big, but I didn't."

Instantly the smile left my face. "Big?" I repeated in disbelief. "Me?" I'd known winning the contest had made me feel special. But I certainly hadn't thought I'd acted *big*. "Why did they think that?"

The girl shrugged. "I don't know. Besides, it wasn't you as much as the pretty one. You know, the one with all the collars."

I rolled my eyes. How stupid. Just because you're finally popular for once in your life . . . just because people point at you admiringly . . . that doesn't mean you're acting big!

I tried to calm myself down by looking out the window. Fern was just getting on the bus. She had her ceramic beaver in one hand and her letter in the other. Typically, the seat behind the driver was still empty, so she carefully set her things down and slid in next to the window. I remembered when I had been sitting next to her in the same seat. It had only been two weeks before, but so much had happened, it seemed like forever.

"Don't look at her, Dinah!" commanded my brain. "It's her own fault she has to sit with Bucky. Besides, if she sees you looking, she'll probably throw another fit."

I turned back to look outside again. Marilyn and Cassandra were gone, and not being able to see them made me feel sort of sad. I wished I had taken more time to say good-bye.

Just then the bus engines started, and we were on our way. It was a different bus driver, but we had only gone a mile or two before he reached for his microphone. Practically the whole bus moaned at once.

"Testing. Testing . . . one, two, three . . . testing."

"No songs!" shouted two girls from the back.

We didn't have to worry. He didn't turn out to be anything like Bernard.

"We'll be arriving at our destination in approximately fifty minutes. I expect all of you to be quiet and behave yourselves. Noise makes me nervous, and I'd really hate to crash this bus."

I never thought I'd say this, but I liked Bernard better.

Up front, Fern never turned around. She just sat and stared out the window. I wish I could have kept myself from looking at her, but my eyes are a very disobedient part of my body. They almost never listen to a thing my brain tells them to do. Whenever someone throws up at school, no matter how fast the rest of me tries to rush by, my eyes always try to sneak a peek. Scientists ought to do some research on this problem.

Anyway, the more my eyes insisted on staring at Fern, the more uncomfortable I became. It was sort of like staring at a sloppy room. It's not so bad if you just breeze in and out and not pay much attention to it. But if you're sitting in the middle of the mess for an hour, you keep getting the feeling that you should be *doing* something about it. You don't always do it, but you always feel like you should.

That's what it was like to ride home with Fern that day on the bus. Seeing her sit there all alone with that stupid little beaver was more than I could stand. I tried to get mad again. But sometimes getting mad takes a lot of energy. And I guess I had gotten tired of trying.

"Excuse me!" I said, jumping up from my seat. "I've got to go talk to someone."

I didn't wait for the girl next to me to move her legs. I didn't wait for anything. It was another one of those spur-of-the-moment decisions that I just had to follow through on.

As I was hurrying up the aisle, the bus driver spotted me in his rearview mirror.

"Shoo!" he said, flailing his arm at me. "Go back and take your seat! Shoo!"

He was treating me like a stray animal. If Marilyn had been there, I'm sure she would have gotten his badge number or whatever it is you get when you report a bus driver. But not being that bold, I quickly lowered myself to the edge of the seat next to Fern.

"Don't scream, Fern," I blurted as her eyes opened wide in surprise. "Please don't scream. I'm not sure why I'm here yet myself, but as soon as I figure out what to say, you'll be the first to know. Meanwhile, just don't scream."

Fern snatched Bucky off the scat and turned her back to me.

"Look. I *know* I did something horrible to you. And

128

I *know* it won't make any difference now. But I want you to know that I'm sorry for pushing you out of the canoe, Fern. *Really* sorry."

"Sure you are," she snapped, still not looking at me.

"I *am*, Fern. I know I had no right to treat you that way. I've never done anything like that before. Not ever. You don't have to believe me, but it's true. I've never pushed *anyone* out of *anything*. Not even my sister, if you can believe that."

Fern didn't respond.

I took a deep breath. "I just don't want you to hate me, Fern. That's all. I'm not a bad person, and I just don't want to be hated."

"I can't help it," came the reply in a voice much louder than before. It sounded shaky, as if she was trying hard not to lose control.

"You mean you hate me?"

Fern turned angrily in my direction. There were tears in her eyes. "I thought you'd be different, but you weren't. You were just like all the others. You think that just because you're popular, you're better than—"

"But I'm not!" I interrupted. "I'm *not* popular! Not usually, that is. Usually I'm just like you."

Fern snorted and wiped her runny nose on her sleeve.

"Well, not *exactly* like you," I corrected. "But close. Very close. And even if I weren't, it wouldn't have given me the right to push you overboard like I did. I know that now."

But then I paused for a second and sighed. "Who

am I trying to kid? I knew it *then,* too. I knew it all along."

Suddenly Fern took a deep breath and shivered slightly. She didn't look as angry as before. She just looked sort of tired. Or maybe sad. Whatever it was, she didn't argue anymore. She just wiped the tears off her face and turned back toward the window.

"Go away," she muttered.

Stunned, I sat there while "Go away" echoed loudly in my head. I'm not sure what I had expected. "Don't worry about it," maybe, or "It's okay." But I never expected not to be forgiven.

I'm not sure how long I stayed there before I went back to my seat. I don't even remember going. Things like that happen sometimes when you're stunned. Time passes, and you miss it completely. The next thing I knew, we were pulling into the bus stop.

I didn't see Fern again. Not face to face, I mean. But since she was the first one off the bus, I watched through the window as her mother ran to greet her. It wasn't hard to pick Ilsa out of the crowd. She was the only mother there wearing a beret and a T-shirt that said BEAM ME UP, SCOTTY. I guess it was funny, but even now, it doesn't make me laugh.

Hubby was there too. I didn't get a good look at him, but he looked nice. As nice as someone can look from the back, that is. He hugged Fern for a long time.

I sat and looked out my window until everyone else was off the bus. I probably would have sat there even longer, but the bus driver came down the aisle and told me to move it.

When I looked up, my mother was peeking inside the doorway, and my father was next to her yelling, "There she is! There she is!"

As soon as the two of them got their hands on me, they started hugging and kissing me so much you would have thought I had been missing for years. The strange thing was, it didn't embarrass me at all. I guess it felt so good to be loved, there wasn't time for embarrassment.

Deena had come to welcome me too. But she hadn't bothered to get out of the car. I think it was her way of saying she was glad to see me, but not *that* glad.

Her greeting, when I got in the car, was typical. "Hi, squirt. Phew! You smell like you haven't had a bath in weeks!"

"Hello, Deena," I replied smugly. "Nice to see you, too."

Wanda was waiting at my house when we got there. I think she was a little bit embarrassed about it. She said she just happened to be walking past, but I didn't really buy that. She still had marks on the backs of her legs from sitting on the curb till we arrived.

I had wondered how I would feel when I saw her again. After all, she certainly wasn't as pretty as Cassandra Leigh Barnhill or as funny as Marilyn Powers. But as soon as she ran to greet me, I knew I didn't want her to be any of those things. I just wanted her to be

Wanda. And it was so good to be with her again, I couldn't stop grinning. New friends are nice. But old friends are just so *easy*. . . .

When we walked through the front door, I breathed in the familiar smell of my house—mostly a combination of Deena's smelly perfumes and Rollo. Neither of these is very pleasant alone, but when they get mixed up with the smells from the kitchen, it comes out kind of nice. Better than Wanda's house, anyway. Wanda's mother is a cleaning freak, and the place always smells like a pine forest.

Once we were inside, everyone seemed to go in a different direction. Mom and Dad each carried a load of dirty clothes directly to the washer. "Hurry!" joked Dad. "Before they begin to multiply!"

I'm not sure where Deena went. All I heard was a "Ta ta. Gotta dash!" It was strange, but for the first time ever, I didn't feel the slightest bit jealous. I'd had all the dashing I wanted for a while.

Wanda and I headed for my room, where I immediately plopped down on my bed. Wanda picked up my arm and looked at my wrist. "Are you blood brothers with anyone?" she teased, sounding a little self-conscious. "Make any good friends?"

"Good? Are you kidding? They were great!"

Then I leaned over and playfully rumpled her hair. "But not as great as you, of course."

Wanda made a face and smoothed out her hair. "Well, if I'm still your best friend, then you must remember how I hate having my hair messed up," she said. I could tell she was trying not to sound relieved.

I laughed. "Sorry, kiddo."

"I also hate being called kiddo."

"How 'bout Buffy or Bunny?"

"Buffy or Bunny? What are you talking about?" she asked.

"Tell you later," I said. "Right now, why don't we go down to the kitchen and get something to eat? You wouldn't *believe* some of the stuff I've actually swallowed the past two weeks. I'm not kidding, Wanda. Most of it just sort of slithered down your throat, whether you wanted it to or not."

Wanda made a face. "Gross. It sounds like the egg my grandmother made me this morning. She never cooks that slime stuff on top."

The two of us started to laugh. "How'd you like a bologna and lettuce sandwich on whole wheat?" I suggested. "It'll be nice to know what's between the bread for a change."

"Since when do we know what's in bologna?" asked Wanda. "My father says bologna is one of life's great mysteries."

I put my arm around her shoulder and marched her down to the kitchen, where Mom was setting the table. Rollo was waiting at the back door. He had slobbered all over the screen, but my mother was surprisingly nice about it.

"Oh, go ahead and let him in for a few minutes to say hello. After all, this is a special occasion," she said cheerfully.

133

Normally, Rollo doesn't get to come in the house during the day. It's pretty hard for Mom to watch him drool and shed all over the carpet without screaming a lot.

After I let him in and hugged him, I stood up to make the sandwiches.

"Er . . . ah . . . would you mind boiling your hands before you touch my bread?" asked Wanda meekly. "I mean, I like Rollo and everything, but it never hurts to be on the safe side."

I punched her on the arm and pretended to be insulted. But after a few seconds I couldn't help but smile. It was nice being home again.

There are a lot of things about home that you take for granted. It's not until you go away for a while that you really appreciate them. Old friends are a perfect example. Clean sheets and soft toilet paper are two more. Even Fern would probably agree with me there.

I still think about Fern a lot. I don't think I'll ever forget about what I did to Fern Wadley.

I tried to call her once. I don't know why. No one answered. I have no idea what I would have done if Fern had said hello. Probably just hung up.

Maybe I'll send her a Christmas card this year. If I do, I think I'll get her one of those religious ones. I figure it'd be pretty difficult for her to hate me while she's looking at a manger scene. Just to be on the safe side, maybe I won't sign my name.

I'll always wish she had forgiven me. Forgiveness

makes guilt a lot easier to handle. But I guess I won't blame her if she never does. One of these days, though, I'm going to stop blaming myself. It hasn't happened yet. I still feel ashamed when I think about her. But I'm going to try. Eventually, you've *got* to forgive yourself for the stuff you do wrong or you'll go crazy.

I read something like that in a book one time. It was part of an assignment we had to read for science, about puberty and stuff. It said that you can't expect yourself to always do the right thing and never mess up. It also said that it's okay to make mistakes sometimes if you can learn from them.

I still have the poster that says DINAH FEENEY—THE KIND ONE. It's in the back of my closet. When I got home from camp, I thought about throwing it away. After all, I'm sure there are lots of people around who would think it's false advertising. Deena would, of course. And Fern. . . .

Besides, Wanda was right when she said it didn't have enough zip to it. I know it'll never win an election. But even so, sometimes in the morning when I get dressed for school, I catch a glimpse of it back there, and it makes me feel good. Even if it *is* false advertising, it never hurts to have a little kindness tucked away somewhere.

And anyway, even after everything that happened, I still sort of like the sound of it. DINAH FEENEY—THE KIND ONE. Maybe I shouldn't. But I do.